Cultivated Pleasures

Cultivated Pleasures

The Art of Romantic Gardening

Photography by: Jacqui Hurst

Text by: Elizabeth Saft

Consulting Editor: Kim Freeman

VIKING STUDIO BOOKS

VIKING STUDIO BOOKS

Published by the Penguin Group
Viking Penguin Inc., 40 West 23 Street,
New York, New York 10010, U.S.A.
Penguin Books Ltd, 27 Wrights Lane,
London W8 5TZ, England
Penguin Books Australia Ltd, Ringwood,
Victoria, Australia
Penguin Books Canada Ltd, 2801 John Street,
Markham, Ontario, Canada L3R 1B4
Penguin Books (N.Z.) Ltd, 182-190 Wairau Road,
Auckland 10, New Zealand
Penguin Books Ltd, Registered Offices:
Harmondsworth, Middlesex, England

First published 1989 by Viking Penguin Inc.

Published simultaneously in Canada

Photographs by Jacqui Hurst: © Jacqui Hurst, 1989
Photographs by other contributors:
Kate Zari: pages: 4-5, 12-13, 19, 30, 36, 49, 88-89, 91, 110-111,
113, 136, 139b, 142t, 144-145, 151t, 163tr, 167
Copyright © Kate Zari, 1989
Kim Freeman pages: 171, 179
Copyright © Kim Freeman, 1989
John Smallwood pages: 35, 48, 120, 158t, 165r
Copyright © John Smallwood, 1989
Bill Stites pages: 195, 209
Courtesy Bill Stites
t: top; b: bottom; l: left; r: right

LIBRARY OF CONGRESS CATALOGING IN PUBLICATION DATA
Saft, Elizabeth
Cultivated pleasures.
1. Gardening. 2. Indoor gardening. I. Freeman, Kim
II. Hurst, Jacqui. III. Title.
SB450.97.S34 1989   635.9   88-40392
ISBN0–670–82269–8

PRODUCED BY SMALLWOOD & STEWART,
9 WEST 19TH ST., NEW YORK, N.Y. 10011

Designed by Sue Rose   Printed in Italy

Contents

Introduction

ABOVE: *Neatly-trimmed hedges border a daisy-studded walk leading towards a distant eighteenth-century English manor.*

RIGHT: *Drifts of naturalized daffodils are one of the most welcome signs in the garden, confirming that spring has come. As long as the grass can be left uncut until both flowers and leaves have faded, daffodils will quickly multiply to produce a woodland effect.*

omance and gardens are a natural pair, each creating its own world wherever it may be, transforming the mundane into the sublime. So, "romantic gardening" is perhaps a redundancy: is not any cultivated haven of flowers and shrubs, trees and water, pathways and garden seats inherently entrancing? The fascination of nature bent to man's desire—whether as a rectangular reflecting pond or masses of flowers tumbling over each other in a small cottage garden—encourages most anyone's fantasy of the bucolic life, lived in perfect harmony with earth and seasons, free from burdensome day-to-day cares.

Each age and generation creates its own idea of the romantic garden: the Persians through enclosed water gardens that were cool respites from their arid climate; the ancient Chinese in naturalistic landscapes full of poetic allusions to the beauty of Nature; the court of Versailles in sweeping formal gardens that epitomized the supreme majesty of the King. Closer to our own era, the early Victorians were fascinated by the exotic discoveries of the plant hunters and by the new inventions for the garden, such as the greenhouse and the lawn mower. In massive hothouses, Victorian gardeners carefully raised tender annuals from all parts of the world for planting in immense, brightly-colored patterns that were as busy and ornate as any high-Victorian parlor. In this century, we have turned away from formality and embraced a more naturalistic approach in our choice of plants and their design. Many of the most influential gardens have been inspired in part by the unassuming virtues of the traditional English cottage garden while still drawing on a diversity of influences and styles.

What is romance but the ideal? Romance is whatever is not quotidian: whatever lifts one out of the habits and preoccupations of daily life to a world of higher, more sensual pleasures. And yet there is a certain horticultural style which does seem to focus on the dreamy, fantastic aspects of barely controlled plant life, which responds to emotional impulses rather than to architectural ideas of nature shaped into building material. This is what most late-twentieth-century garden lovers would most likely call romantic. We, like the late Victorians, who lived in the shadow of the Industrial Revolution, cohabit with the miracles and miseries of modern technology, and thus long for nature triumphant and man subdued.

RIGHT: *At Old Westbury Gardens, New York, a double perennial bed planted with dahlias, chrysanthemums, and daisies acts as a foil for the formal and quite imposing garden.*

14

ABOVE: *Parnham House in Dorset dates from 1540, and its gardens have been extensively (and lavishly) restored. Trimmed to play up their wooly texture, these majestic yews are rich ornamentation throughout the seasons.*

The following pages contain a wide variety of gardens, both indoors and out, chosen simply for their sheer power to allure, inspire, and transport their admirers. They are contemporary romantic gardens, places where the gardener or designer has played out his or her fantasies. While they do have certain things in common, no hard-and-fast rules have been observed. Anything that beguiles and seduces is romantic, and we have chosen these simply because they captivated us and powerfully conveyed their creators' dreams.

But if any one attribute had to be chosen as most important to gardening pleasure, both for the gardener and the garden visitors, perhaps it should be playfulness. It is the willingness to challenge the rules when they don't serve to realize one's dream garden; to produce one's own creation (and make mistakes while doing so) rather than follow a color-by-numbers garden designer's plan; to experiment with techniques, juxtapositions, and effects; and while doing this, to find pleasure in the process (which can be never-end-

ing in the garden). Whimsy and delight make a garden come to life. They allow for the personal stamp of the gardener, and for serendipitous effects to come into being. Romantic gardeners do not take themselves or their gardens too seriously, for of course, romance is long gone once duty arrives.

The romantic gardener is a dreamer first of all, and a realist only when absolutely necessary. He or she derives inspiration from the natural shapes, colors, and scents of favored plants and would like most of all to see nature run rampant in a completely approachable manner, as if wisteria and rose, grass and water, wood and stone conspired together to create a perfectly habitable retreat.

At heart, all who love gardens are romantics, for the creation of a beautiful garden is essentially a romantic endeavor in which, as with a long love affair, imagination and whimsy, knowledge and fervor, faith and plain hard work are joined to create the illusion of effortless and natural perfection.

ABOVE: *To create a sense of wilderness at the edge of their New York garden, the owners left tall borders of pink clover and ox-eye daisies to spill over the rough-mown grass path.*

16

RIGHT: *Inspired by a Japanese print, Monet designed a single-span bridge over the lily pond he built and later painted so many times at Giverny. Wisteria rambles across its railings, casting pale reflections of its hanging racemes in the water below. On the banks are thick plantings of sweet-scented meadowsweet (*Filipendula Ulmaria*) and broad-leafed butterbur (*Petasites japonicus*).*

ABOVE: *In midsummer, the bold colors of snapdragons in a vase or floating in a bowl bring a moody accent to a city windowsill.*

ABOVE: *Imagination can find space for a homemade garden almost anywhere. Glass containers of grass and a bottle of daisies and Queen Anne's Lace brighten the gritty ledge of a city property.*

RIGHT: *Blending the perimeter of a garden with its surroundings is an effective means of preserving a sense of romantic seclusion. Here, New York landscape architect Randolph Marshall constructed a naturalistic waterfall that merges a swimming pool into the bordering woodland.*

ABOVE: *Lavatera, poppies, coreopsis, and bright pink* Lychnis coronaria *fill a country garden border.*

LEFT: *A warm, repetitive pink and lavender color scheme unifies the terraced beds in a Gloucestershire manor house, making the property seem less awesome.*

Inspirations

When gardeners look for inspiration and ideas it seems only natural to turn to the great gardens of history. Although gardens are a transitory medium subject to the process of growth and decay more than almost any other art, through restoration and research we can learn what gardens of the past were like. At places like Villa Lante, near Rome, we can discover a theatrical mix of wit and classical themes in a terraced Renaissance water garden; at Williamsburg, Virginia, we can learn what it feels like to walk through an early eighteenth-century garden.

We can look to the styles of eighteenth- and nineteenth-century England for the closest antecedents of our present-day notions of romantic gardening. For years, English gardening had been modeled on the formal and highly stylized Dutch and French gardens. At Versailles, André Le Nôtre created a garden whose monumental scale and artificial style expressed the power and reach of the French ruling class. Spacious terraces decorated with a series of parterres near the palace looked over several thousand acres of formally-planted trees. This vast expanse of geometric greenery was crisscrossed with wide, straight paths that served to exaggerate the orderliness and panoramic sweep of the garden, and dotted with fountains and pools and statuary.

This rigid, autocratic style became anathema to a group of English garden designers who, at the beginning of the eighteenth century, began to take their cues from the so-called Romantic painters and writers—Claude Lorrain, Nicolas Poussin, and Alexander Pope. The Romantics saw man as subservient to Nature, and Nature a raging and unpredictable creature whose very capriciousness was the heart of her attraction. Nature, whether human or Mother, would win out over all, and there was a deep and fearsome thrill in surrendering oneself to whatever natural impulses beat in one's breast. Rejecting the classical requirements of strict form, in horticulture and in literature, the Romantics dreamt of craggy peaks and thundering cataracts, of the exaltation of the sense in every realm.

When in the 1730s William Kent began to design gardens, most notably at Stowe, English garden design became more *dégagé* than ever before and the art of landscape design (or "landskip," as it was then called) was born. Kent favored broad vistas of lawn and forest which were designed to seem natural, with expanses of water

RIGHT: *The sweeping branches of a magnificent cedar of Lebanon are nature's counterpoint to the classical columns of an eighteenth-century portico.*

ABOVE: *The strong, sculptural forms of most topiary often demand that all other plantings be equally emphatic. In the blue garden at Crathes Castle, Scotland, a mass of deep blue cornflowers is planted in front of the dark yew hedges.*

and architectural follies to anchor the eye. He deliberately blurred the delineation between wilderness and garden and created scenes in which the hand of man was disguised. These new landscapes were Nature perfected or domesticated. By mowing down acres of trees one could create a vista that enhanced what remained; by changing the slope of a hill, by adding a mount, by digging a pond, one could intensify the feeling of being in the heart of Nature. "Ruined" temples and gazebos and their like simply underscored the point that Nature eventually claims all for her own.

"Capability" Brown, the reigning monarch of landscape and garden design in England during the second half of the eighteenth

ABOVE: *It is not hard to be lulled by the lush plantings and use of color in Monet's garden at Giverny. Here red, pink, and white peonies, white and pale-lilac stocks, and red and orange roses line a path.*

century, was a great destroyer of the parterres and topiary of the old French- and Dutch-influenced formal gardens that graced the stately homes of England. Like Kent, he was a fervent proponent of naturalistic landscapes, most of which included large expanses of water, many with gurgling falls or scenic streams. The work of these two men and others like them released the English, who were now the foremost gardeners of the Western world, from the requirements of strict formalism, and eventually led to the sensuous styles we now think of as romantic. Liberated from the autocratic aesthetic of Versailles, Kent and Brown showed that gardeners should turn to Nature for inspiration rather than dictate to it.

ABOVE: *Ingenuity brings an entirely new dimension to a tiny backyard in Brooklyn, New York, as climbers like these sweet peas have been encouraged to take over two old wooden ladders.*

RIGHT: *Treating an existing pond as the organizing element, New York landscape architects Stewart Associates enhanced a bucolic setting with plantings of purple loosestrife, grasses, and cattails. The artless and natural-looking result seems almost to deny the design's careful planning and attention to detail.*

ABOVE: *In the winter landscape, the garden assumes a more limited palette and profile. Gilded in snow, trees, buildings, fences, and paths—the bones of the garden—rise to prominence.*

LEFT: *Autumn brings a new palette to the garden and, as the flowers die away, trees and garden architecture assume greater importance. At the top of this steep, wooded hill, a white gazebo will be the focal point until next spring.*

RIGHT: *Snowdrops are almost late-winter rather than early-spring plants, appearing even when patches of snow still cover the garden.*

32

LEFT: *The colors and textures found in fresh vegetables and fruits naturally complement those of fresh flowers. Combined, they can make eye-catching, beautiful centerpieces for the kitchen or dining table.*

BELOW: *Height is especially important in the cramped spaces of small city gardens and can be introduced with climbers such as sweet peas and roses, by using hanging baskets, or by stacking containers behind each other.*

RIGHT: *Tall daylilies and grasses and
busy borders of low-growing daisies,
geraniums, and blue dwarf campanula
on a New York City penthouse designed
by landscape gardener Lisa Stamm
soften a view of city rooftops.*

Two late-Victorian gardeners were the next great influences on romantic gardening: William Robinson and Gertrude Jekyll. Victorian gardens were generally highly formal places planted with hundreds, sometimes thousands, of fragile hothouse annuals in elaborate designs modeled on oriental carpets and other intricate patterns described in garden books of the day.

Jekyll and Robinson abhorred this contrivance: plants that survived only because of the proximity of a greenhouse, designs that were rigid and unnatural, plants or color combinations that did not occur in nature. In books and articles, Robinson aggressively championed the virtues of wildflowers and indigenous plants in the garden and turned the emphasis of the gardener to the plant material itself. Trained as a painter, Jekyll brought a highly refined eye to her garden schemes, advocating a naturalistic scheme and use of color in her long, wide perennial borders.

Jekyll's use of color, which depended on harmonies and gradual progressions from shade to shade, her love for what actually occurs in Nature, and her appreciation of the artless charm of the English cottage garden still form the basis of many of our contemporary notions of the romantic garden.

Like all artists, gardeners turn to the classics of their field for instruction and inspiration, and aspire to create gardens as successful in their own right as are the masterpieces of the art. But it is both thrilling and disheartening to peruse truly grand gardens. Those of international fame, such as the spectacular azalea gardens at Bellingrath, Alabama, or the perennial borders at Hidcote, England, can have a confounding effect. We are thrilled with the sheer beauty and artistry of a magnificent garden and then inevitably disheartened: turning back to our own modest plot and limited means, we wonder how it is possible to capture even a fraction of the magic and inspiration of the masterpieces of garden design.

Great gardens should not be viewed as blueprints or even reproach, but as points of departure from which to derive one's own unique ideas for an entirely original, private paradise. Discovering an unusual plant or a successful combination of textures or colors in a border, a decorative pattern of bricks in a wall, or an edging for a path can provide ideas or solutions to adapt and translate into our own private Edens.

ABOVE: *A south-facing terrace in the middle of Manhattan takes full advantage of its location by training clematis along its railings.*

TOP LEFT: *A white color scheme using trailing 'Sea Foam' roses, Queen Anne's Lace, and chamomile around a dry stone wall and an arch calms an otherwise wild corner of a garden.*

BELOW LEFT: *The dramatic qualities of an entrance can be heightened with hints of the garden beyond. Here, an arched entrance to a walled rose garden becomes more enticing when it is framed with hollyhocks and pale yellow roses, 'Leverkusen.'*

After wallowing in the consummate glory of an exquisite garden, the amateur gardener needs to take a step back, a deep breath, and begin to sort out the effects and pleasures of such a work of art. For a successful garden arises both from an overall impression and a series of sublime vignettes. Concentrating on these vignettes helps to give clues as to how the whole is created, and also provides manageable ideas for one's own endeavor.

All gardens must have their origins in the qualities of their site—Pope's "genius of place." This was one of the great achievements of the eighteenth-century gardens of Brown and Kent. They understood that a garden must capitalize on the virtues of the landscape and the same is true for any successful romantic garden. Plainly, a garden with a beautiful view should emphasize and use that view, not screen or distract from it with heavy plantings. A hillside garden can employ a series of terraces to create several different but related "rooms." Inspiration can also be derived from restriction. Apartment dwellers might focus on window boxes, creating strong color combinations to draw the eye and maximize the impact of a small collection of plants. Or, the gardener in a small city garden might enclose still further, planting densely to create tiny, secluded areas and emphasize the sense of a verdant sanctuary.

In small gardens, scale is important—one wants the feeling of being overwhelmed but not claustrophobic, and the garden should not be dominated by one large tree or group of plants. So, in the same way, an awareness of scale is necessary when devising a scheme for any size garden or any house. The great eighteenth-century gardeners were designing for the great classical mansions of their day—architecture of a scale and grandeur that could stand amid the vistas they created. Jekyll and Robinson's style of gardening, because it took so much of its inspiration from cottage gardens, can work on a smaller scale. (Even so, most of the gardens they designed were far larger than most people own or can afford to maintain today.)

LEFT: *Long perennial beds line both entrances to the pergola at Old Westbury Gardens, New York, and lattice-work pagodas heighten the sense that the visitor is entering a special part of the garden.*

Within a garden, scent and color are two great tools at the disposal of the romantic gardener. Site and scale are usually givens that must be worked with, but the use of scent and color is something within the gardener's control. Because it has extraordinary power to transport and evoke, touching us in a profound way, scent is essential to any romantic garden. Without it, an entire dimension of our experience of a garden is lost. It is always a disappointment to bend down and smell an exquisitely colored flower to discover that it has no fragrance. This is frequently the complaint with many of the new hybrids, especially roses, which have been bred for some novel or ever more intense color and have lost their scent in the process.

We are always handicapped in discussing scent because we lack the vocabulary or memory that we have for colors or shapes. Scent varies from the extreme sweetness of jasmine, hyacinth, or honeysuckle, each of which is different in its own way, to the spicy/sweet scent of some roses, or to the more astringent aromas of pine trees or eucalyptus. But though we may not be able to classify scents adequately, most gardeners discover their favorites and for them, no garden is complete without including a display of those plants.

Scent, especially the more delicate examples, can be elusive, so it is always best to plant scented flowers, shrubs, or trees close to the places that are most popular in a garden, such as walkways and seats, or beneath windows so that breezes will carry the scent indoors. A footpath edged with lavender or rambling old-fashioned roses around the front door will ensure that the house is filled with intoxicating perfumes every time a visitor arrives.

Some plants release their scent only when crushed: in cottage gardens, herbs like thyme and chamomile, rosemary and mint, often spill over onto the paths not just because this makes them easier to pick but also because they release their scent as they are brushed against by passersby.

But while scent has such great power, it is not as lasting as color, which shapes our first impressions of most gardens year-round. Gertrude Jekyll's exploration and use of color in her gardens remains a paragon for all gardeners. But her border designs contain other lessons, too. She massed plantings to great effect, showing that irregular drifts of the same plant added to its impact.

LEFT: *A pair of antique children's chairs provides just the right pedestals for two bunches of fresh-cut old-fashioned roses. Imaginative still-lifes like this are versatile and interesting ways to display even the simplest flowers.*

ABOVE: *Entrances can be rich with romantic allusions and possibilities. Framed by a dense green hedge, a plain wood-slatted gate appears far more significant.*

While the scale of her herbaceous borders may be absurdly demanding for today's gardener, the grouping of the same or related plants is a technique that can be practiced in any garden. Plainly, the smaller or more delicately colored the plant the greater it benefits from this technique. The tiny blooms of lily-of-the-valley, snowdrops, or violas, for example, demand to be grouped in quantities of a dozen or more, whereas the large blowsy heads of peonies or some of the larger phlox or chrysanthemums do not need such grouping for support. Such luxurious plantings, done well without seeming contrived, can convey the sensuous abundance which lies at the heart of romance. By covering small areas lavishly, dense plantings can also serve to mitigate the frustrations of a young garden. Broad patches of color—a drift of daffodils or a small perennial bed will distract attention from immature plantings or bare spots elsewhere. You'll have to divide and transplant overplanted areas in later years, but remember that a garden is never finished—it evolves constantly with or without the help of a gardener, and a major part of the pleasure is in watching it mature and change.

Again, inspiration can often be found in great gardens: is it the luxuriance of billows of flowers that strikes a romantic chord, or does the tranquillity of some shady green glade appeal more? As always, site will dictate much of what is possible, but even without an eighteenth-century mansion and acres of lawn, a sense of majesty can be encouraged by a judicious choice of plants—a few great specimens, an elegant Japanese maple (*Acer palmatum*) or magnificent lily magnolia (*Magnolia quinquepeta*), for example, will be less demanding and more impressive than a riot of colorful annuals. Equally, a small water garden filled with lilies, a trellis draped with a lilac wisteria, or a beautiful piece of sculpture will add interest and character without requiring a lot of time or space.

Above all, when planning a romantic garden, do not be discouraged: even the professional gardener has had the experience of having a well-planned scheme just not do after it is planted, or a beloved specimen die despite all efforts. More happily, though somewhat rarer, there is the pleasure of having a totally unplanned juxtaposition create a magic effect. Gardening is a process of trial and error, because living things don't always do what people decree. And that is part of the beauty of it all.

ABOVE: *Everlasting sweet peas, apple
trees, and zucchini vines twine around
an arbor.*

Romantic Styles

ABOVE: *Seclusion and mystery are valuable romantic features and here they have been combined by a California gardener in a series of outdoor rooms enclosed by tall hedges of Monterey cypress.*

ABOVE RIGHT: *'Ghislaine de Felignonde' climbs over a garden shed, smothering its roof with scented blooms.*

or the modern gardener, one of the great appeals of the romantic style is that the garden can be informal and idiosyncratic. There are no pattern books or precepts; the romantic gardener can draw freely and imaginatively on whatever styles or plants he or she wishes. In this respect, the romantic garden fits the more eclectic, less rule-bound temperament of the late-twentieth century but this spirit is also better suited practically to the more limited time and resources of the modern gardener. Very often, a romantic approach to the garden benefits if evidence of the hand of the gardener is light, and the overall effect is neither imposing nor contrived. This is something of a blessing in disguise for we no longer have the pool of skilled or affordable labor that previous generations had to tend their gardens. Today, without the demands imposed by a rigid or elaborate design, the romantic gar-

ABOVE: *Benches and other garden furniture deserve as much consideration to their position as that given plants. In a shady spot, half hidden by ferns and broad-leafed hostas, a teak bench is a sheltered and secluded retreat.*

dener is free to create a realistic garden that can more easily be managed and maintained. But while the seemingly artless approach of the romantic garden may ultimately require less time to keep up, it often needs almost as much planning as the more formal gardens of earlier generations.

Today's more modest properties are often in urban areas so that a first requirement is establishing the garden as a retreat from the outside world: increasing privacy with high hedges, fences, or walls that shelter the haven of plants and trees. Enclosing a garden creates an aura of secrecy and, practically speaking, will also muffle street noise and hide from sight a busy road or an ugly building. But equally, a fence or hedge can be designed to frame a beautiful view, effectively incorporating it into the property and visually expanding the boundaries of the garden.

ABOVE: *Like a house, a garden can accommodate various romantic moods. In this English garden, the neat lawn and flower beds near the house are separated from less formal plantings by an old brick wall.*

Inside a romantic garden, the design should enhance a sense of mystery. Where shrubs and trees are planted so that not everything is visible at once, curiosity is aroused, exploration is invited and, in turn, areas to be explored are presented. Smaller compact shrubs, especially evergreens, such as boxwood and yew, or euonymus, berberis, or cotoneaster, which produce colorful foliage or berries, or clumps of some of the taller grasses, are good choices for dividing up an open garden and adding character and interest by the creation of smaller "rooms." A small city yard can actually seem larger if it is planted, but not overwhelmed, with modest-sized trees or shrubs. On a larger property, full-sized "rooms" created by hedges or banks of shrubs will give scope to create very different moods: a secluded grassy glade or a scented garden, a hidden seat for reading or relaxing or a tiny patch of favorite flowers.

Glimpses of the garden, rather than complete views—through a doorway, beyond a trellis, between shrubs—piques curiosity in the visitor. Here, pergolas and lattice bring valuable screening effects for the romantic garden. In particular, lattice work has a playful quality appropriate to such a garden; besides providing sturdy support for climbing plants and vines, it can be constructed in any number of decorative patterns that enhance the everchanging play of light and shade it creates. Older garden books often show a variety of decorative designs for lattice. Similarly, garden structures and buildings—pergolas, loggias, gazebos, and so on—belong in a romantic garden for amusement, not serving a strictly practical purpose but adding to the atmosphere and mood as well as the actual structure of the garden.

As with all successful gardens, good design must begin with the virtues and characteristics of the site itself—the soil, the lay and slope of the land, the situation of the house, the progress of the sun across the property each day, and the existing trees and features. A large outcrop of bare rock or a steep slope, for instance, is part of the texture of a property and can be incorporated perhaps in a more informal design or wild garden. Similarly, an existing stand of trees can become a focal point for a property.

Often overlooked in planning a garden is the importance of the view from within the house—from upstairs and down as well as from porches and verandas. This is how the garden will be viewed

RIGHT: *A shady corner includes an early nineteenth-century urn and plinth. A circular carpet of white daisies forms a floral base and blends the formal container into the surrounding garden.*

BELOW: *When plantings or architectural elements are used as focal points, the eye can be led through a garden, enhancing the feeling of space. This garden has a series of areas, from the overgrown path in the foreground to an enclosed lily pond, then to the perennial border in the middle distance and finally ending at the yew topiary.*

RIGHT: *In a witty reference to classical tradition, designer Karl Mann used an avenue of pleached evergreens at the end of his Long Island garden to create a dramatic stage for an eighteenth-century bust.*

most frequently, throughout the day and evening, and throughout the seasons. With this consideration, one or two flowering trees should be placed so that they can be seen from the windows of the kitchen or the comfort of the sitting room, or scented flowers and shrubs positioned beneath windows or near the front door so that summer breezes will bring their perfumes into the house.

On a larger scale, garden architecture and the lines formed by paths and hedges, and the shapes formed by large plantings, create the strong substructure of any garden, most visible from above or in winter. Medieval gardeners understood the importance of this: their parterres were designed to be looked down upon from the house. To modern taste, the symmetry and rigid form of the parterre does not belong in a romantic garden; irregularity and ordered confusion are valuable romantic effects. But, as in any garden, some structure must lie beneath the ordering of textures and colors; randomly setting a collection of favorite plants would create only disturbing chaos.

BELOW: *A simple entrance in a picket fence is emphasized here by a pair of pink polyanthas, 'The Fairy.' They are repeat bloomers that will add color late in the season.*

LEFT: *Color adds much to our impressions of a garden. In an informal garden, it provides direction and shape to an overgrown brick path, as masses of wild pink geraniums converge on an arbor of white roses.*

RIGHT: *The hardy groundcover blue star creeper (*Laurentia Fluviatilis*) grows in soft pillows around the rough stone steps leading to the lily pond of a California garden.*

For many of us, a wild garden epitomizes the romantic. Of course, such a garden is not wild at all but cultivated to appear so and carefully designed to make the most of the more delicate forms of wild flowers. But the result should share the informal virtues of a natural meadow or roadside. In an alarmingly short space of time wild flowers that used to grow freely along our roadsides have been disappearing and many of the plants we took for granted have become endangered. Wild gardens draw on this plant material, and so have the virtue of contributing towards the conservation of our fragile heritage of native flowers.

RIGHT: *Thriving under benign neglect, daffodils create a garden as timeless as it is cheerful. The bulbs have been naturalized; that is, planted to appear as they would in a wild garden.*

A wild garden is not the "low-maintenance garden" so desired by many but does require some time and skilled work. Before planting, the soil has to be thoroughly dug over and weeds and grasses that would compete with wild flowers removed. Poor soil is actually better for a wild garden because it discourages competitors. Indigenous plantings may be preferable not just for their look or their ecological values, but also for their great tenacity. In marshy or waterlogged ground, windy seashore or rocky soil, they may be the only plants that will gain a firm foothold.

In a wild garden, much of the romance comes from the simple charms of these most unpretentious flowers—the native plants and grasses of the surrounding countryside. The flowers and plants should be scattered and strewn about the garden, among the rocks, in crevices in the paths, and in the grass, as if by nature. Consequently wild gardens need to be separated from built-up areas, where they seem contrived. Many properties surrounded by trees, for example, can support woodland-style gardens with native plants and shrubs along their paths and in cleared glades. In a woodland garden, native American flowering shrubs such as mountain laurel (*Kalmia latifolia*), nannyberry (*Viburnum lentago*), rosebay rhododendron (*Rhododendron maximum*), and low-bush blueberry (*Vaccinium augustifolium*) will provide color. Native wild flowers such as the white wood anemone (*Anemone quinquefolia*), yellow-green jack-in-the-pulpit (*Arisaema triphyllum*), pink lady's slipper (*Cypripedium acaule*), and russet yellow trout lily (*Erythronium americanum*) will thrive on a woodland floor.

The random massing of flowers in a wild garden style is seen most often (and most effectively) in the naturalized drifts of daffodils, crocuses, snowdrops, and other early bulbs that bring their gloriously refreshing colors to the muted palette of the garden in the first weeks of spring. This style of planting can be continued through summer with a careful selection of later-blooming plants, to create a meadow-like effect in the unmown grass. Foxglove, primula, snakeshead fritillary, poppy, sweet pea, wild rose, wild sweet william, cornflower, columbine, loosestrife, wild geranium, larkspur, and crested iris are some of the most popular wild flowers, each displaying a delicacy characteristic of non-hybridized plants.

Cutting the meadow perhaps only twice during the summer—sometime in May and again in late September will preserve the wild effect for as long as possible. Where desired, paths can be mown through the high grass to create walks and contrasting areas of interest, while around the house or closer to more formal areas the grass can be kept short for practical purposes.

Wildflower gardens are rich in shelter and sustenance and naturally attract birds, bees, butterflies and other forms of wildlife. Different species of butterflies feed on different plants. But wildflowers such as ox-eye daisies (*Chrysanthemum leucanthemum*), common honeysuckle (*Lonicera periclymenum*), sunflowers (*Helianthus annus*), and the common dandelion (*Tarazacum officinale*) will attract butterflies with their nectar. Michaelmas daisies, red valerian, scented old-fashioned roses, and of course the butterfly bush (*Buddleia davidii*) are among the more popular garden plants that draw butterflies to the garden.

ABOVE: *Lavender and yellow St. John's Wort and senecio seem perfectly at home in a 'wild garden.' Combined, they form a vivid border for pathways or low cover for slopes.*

LEFT: *In a wild garden in England composed entirely of plants which predate Victorian times, columbines (*Aquilegia vulgaris*) play a central role by supplying a jolt of color amid unmown grass.*

LEFT: *In a wild garden, virtually any spot is suitable for planting. Hardy prostrate varieties should be allowed to invade footpaths; walls will provide a foothold for ferns, mosses, or a Welsh poppy.*

BELOW: *Planting thickly and mixing a great variety of herbs and wild flowers enhance the appeal of this Victorian garden. Old stone containers are filled to the brim with smaller alpine plants, columbines, sweet rocket, and dozens of different herbs.*

RIGHT: *Butterfly gardens are consistently entertaining, even if bees sometimes do come along uninvited. This garden attracts butterflies with its carpet of columbines, foxgloves, chives, dandelions, thistles, and scented herbs—an altogether glorious mix of textures.*

ABOVE: *Lady's mantle (*Alchemilla vulgaris*) is justly popular in cottage gardens. It will grow almost anywhere that is moist, self-seeding vigorously to cover paths or walls with its broad leaves and yellow-green flowers.*

LEFT: *Dark purple buddleia (*Buddleia davidii*) is a fragrant and relatively undemanding covering for a garden building. Below, geraniums, begonias, and nicotiana flourish in a stone urn.*

FAR LEFT: *A colorful chaos of white and pink foxgloves and ivory roses isolates and seems almost to overwhelm the house. This type of garden belies the considerable planning that precedes it.*

LEFT AND RIGHT: *Cottage gardens can comfortably mix formal and informal aspects in their design. Clipped myrtle and a pair of junipers frame the lower windows and french doors of a thatched house that dates from the early sixteenth-century, while beneath are gray Lamb's Ears (*Stachys byzantina*) and the scarlet floribunda rose 'Sarabande.'*

Unpretentious, colorful, whimsical, innocent . . . the cottage garden conjures up images of a gentler and more benign time, one that is quintessentially romantic. The jumble of old-fashioned plants, spilling out over walks and tumbling around doorways, almost engulfing the house, is truly gardening in the vernacular. To Gertrude Jekyll and William Robinson, the cottage garden was a shining light in the midst of slavish Victorian carpet bedding. At a time when gardens were filled with brightly-colored beds of delicate exotic plants from all over the world that had to be hothouse-raised, Jekyll believed that "one can hardly go into the smallest cottage garden without learning or observing something new." In these tiny gardens, which had evolved over generations, she and Robinson saw the great value of using indigenous plant material in an informal and uncontrived style.

ABOVE: *The deep crimson floribunda 'Dublin Bay' climbs around the front door of this ivy-covered house.*

The sheer exuberance of a cottage garden is hard to resist. This spirit and a gloriously colorful palette give the cottage-garden style a tremendous appeal to the modern non-cottage dweller. Cottage gardens are immensely practical places, for beneath the appearance of benign neglect lies a great deal of sound and frugal gardening, from the use of cuttings and cold frames to raise new plants or extend the growing season by a few weeks to the recycling of vegetable scrapings, leaves, grass cuttings, and hedge clippings in compost to replenish the soil.

Typical cottage garden plants vary since they are so idiosyncratic in style. Plants are allowed to self-seed freely and many are raised from cuttings of favorite varieties in neighbors' gardens. Most cottage gardens, however, would include an assortment of some of the following flowers: hollyhocks, pinks, honeysuckle, old-fashioned roses, foxgloves, wallflowers, stocks, lupines, irises, pyrethrum, poppies, and columbines. A wide variety of vegetables and fruits would be grown for the kitchen, and of course herbs of all kinds for the pot or for pickling, for medicines and balms, sweet bags, pomanders, and potpourris.

ABOVE AND RIGHT: *Dooryard
gardens, window boxes, and hanging
baskets are best when they take a design
lead from the architecture of the house. A
lively clump of daisies gives a casual
welcome to the visitor at the open door of
a modest garden studio. Played against
the walls of an unembellished stone
house, creamy pink hollyhocks soften and
bring warmth to the structure.*

ABOVE: *Sweet peas, valued for their exquisite scent and long-lasting colors, will gaily (and rapidly) overtake almost any support they can find. Supremely abundant, they are marvelous cut flowers for lush indoor bouquets.*

LEFT: *Thyme, rue, sage, savory, and other low-growing herbs carpet a fragrant path to the door of this house. Behind, virginia creeper and clematis 'Perele d'Azure' blanket the walls.*

ABOVE: *Masses of invasive dark pink crane's bill* (Geranium Endresii*) form a luxuriant carpet beneath the heavily fragrant full blooms of 'Madame Isaac Pereire.'*

LEFT: *Lavender, creamy lilies, and spires of dark purple loosestrife crowd an old birdhouse set in view of the open front porch of a Long Island house.*

While the cottage style seemed perfectly in keeping with the modest home it generally surrounded, against a more formal or imposing house the apparent chaos and mix of plants appeared jarring to Jekyll. She wanted to adapt the virtues of the cottage garden, to exploit the great variety of plant material then available in a style suited to larger or more suburban houses.

Developed and perfected by Jekyll, the herbaceous border is founded on the use of perennials and takes full advantage of the tantalizing assortment of flowers that fills the pages of our garden catalogs today. But most of all, it is a style that uses color to full effect. With scent, color is the most powerful mood evoker in the garden and Jekyll mixed and combined colors with a skill and understanding that had not been seen in the garden before. Her first training had been as a painter, and when she turned to gardening later in life, she brought with her an artist's sophisticated sensibility for color and form.

FAR LEFT: *At Crathes Castle, double herbaceous borders converge on a beautifully shaped Portuguese laurel* (Prunus lusitanica). *In early August, astilbe, reddish-orange crocosmia, campanula, and white spires of aconitum are in bloom; the feathery pink plumes of Queen of the Prairie and the bushy gray anthemis form taller focal points and add fragrance to the walk.*

NEAR LEFT: *During late summer when the perennial garden is past its peak, textures play a more important part. Here, broad green leaves of elephant's ears (*Caladium esculentum*) form a lush edging year-round. Opposite, purple catmint spilling over the path creates contrasting textures.*

FAR LEFT: *On a hillside in the Napa Valley, California, dark-blue delphiniums, irises, and white foxgloves create strong vertical accents among masses of pink roses 'Nearly Wild.'*

NEAR LEFT: *Geraniums, daisies, rock roses, and rock garden perennials spill over and around this gravel path in midsummer.*

RIGHT: *In the corner of a vegetable garden, spires of pink salvia (*Salvia turkestanica*) and blue bell-shaped polemonium (*Polemonium foliosissimum*) bloom against the rose-covered brick walls.*

LEFT: *Perennials are the backbone of Monet's garden at Giverny. Near the house, with spring bulbs, violets, and pansies for early color, he planted Japanese anemones, campanulas, and pink stocks. Farther into the garden, there are large drifts of delphiniums, bearded iris, lupines, and phlox in pastel colors accented with deeper hues.*

RIGHT: *Phlox, a cottage garden staple, is also popular in perennial gardens for its fragrance and long blooming period—from midsummer on. In this small garden it is mixed with foxgloves and columbines.*

In a typical perennial garden designed by Jekyll, wide beds of plants are set off against the neutral background of a wall or hedge. Plants are layered towards the back of the bed by height, and their colors are arranged in "drifts": irregularly massed plants of a single color or of several colors, shading harmoniously from one to another. In the herbaceous border, there are no abrupt shifts of color to jar the eye; instead, new colors are introduced by blending one to another gradually. Deeper colors are there to lead the eye, and shrubs or taller plantings act as dividers or accents that separate one area from another. Thus the eye is never fully stopped by the overall scheme.

Jekyll designed many gardens and included countless more planting schemes in her many books for single color gardens, ranging from violet-to-lavender borders to gray or gold borders, or for seasonal effects, such as August and September borders, everywhere mixing color and form with her masterful hand.

For the gardener whose passion is flowers, a perennial bed is irresistible for its satisfying variety of plants. Its design will also mature and develop year after year, whereas a bed of annuals has to be replanted every twelve months. While this makes perennial gardening seem more appealing to today's weekend gardener, in practice the herbaceous border has its own demands. On a Jekyllian scale, it is almost totally impractical for anyone without a team of skilled and diligent gardeners. During the growing season, the processes of staking, pinching back, and weeding are fairly continuous; in spring and autumn, the larger plants will have to be dug up and transplanted or divided.

Most of us, however, are gardening on a more modest scale with a manageable number of plants to care for. From June to September the perennial garden reaches its peak; if the garden is not to appear bare during other months, the perennial gardener will have to add annuals and bulbs to fill in gaps and hide those perennials that have yet to bloom or have finished blooming.

RIGHT: *Acanthus, valued for the strong architectural qualities it brings to a perennial border, can grow three-to four-feet high. Here it frames a sweeping view of surrounding fields and hills.*

ABOVE: *White geraniums add a bright touch to a brick niche in the corner of a shady Manhattan backyard.*

The use of color and mixing of plants in the herbaceous border are still important for the romantic gardener, whose entire flower garden today is probably not much larger than one of Jekyll's large beds and who can give only a few hours a week to its upkeep. Indeed, many gardeners live in towns or cities where containers have to form the urban Eden. On these rooftops and patios, in tiny backyards and city gardens where the soil is too poor, container gardens are a very practical solution. Although there are restrictions—containers do not allow for the same range of plants as a garden and plants are more vulnerable to a sudden frost—container gardening does offer some advantages.

A far greater number of plants can be grown in containers than is generally thought. For the gardener whose tastes tend to the unusual and exotic, the predictable selection of annuals and half-hardy perennials does not create interest or atmosphere. With a good-sized container, boxwood, yew, or red-berried English holly (*Ilex aquifolium*), or winter-blooming laurustinus (*Vibernum tinus*) can flourish. Flanking a front door or at the corners of a patio, these larger plants will add architectural distinction to a space. Dwarf rhododedrons and azaleas, miniature or standard roses, hydrangeas, herbs of all kinds, bulbs, and climbers like clematis, wisteria, and morning glory will all flourish in containers, providing they receive proper care and feeding, frequent watering in dry weather and in winter, protection from freezing.

For a permanent container garden, terracotta or wood or stone is probably better for plants, since these materials "breathe" and allow a natural evaporation of moisture and, with age, they will weather beautifully and blend in with surroundings far better than plastic. In the past, old lead containers, which develop wonderful patina with age, could sometimes be found; but old metal tanks and tubs, and even old stone sinks make good planters, as long as drainage holes can be made.

A great advantage of container gardens is that they can be replanted once the flowers fade, thus keeping up a continuous show of color that can more than compensate for the limited space. But perhaps above all, a container garden is mobile, ready to be moved about to bring emphasis to an entrance, to surround the table for a meal outdoors, or brought inside to brighten a living room or hall.

An old cream-colored stone chimney acts as a pedestal for pots billowing with violet blooms of browallia.

A solitary urn containing bright-red geraniums stands out against a white-painted wall.

Made from natural materials, containers such as this woven basket will weather beautifully.

Deep blue lobelia, red and pink geraniums, and variegated ivy tumble about, forming an urban jungle.

The pale group of Dusty Miller and whites of petunias and impatience temper livelier colors.

Picking up the blue trim on the windows, this bright cushion of lobelia flowers through the summer.

LEFT: *Various pots of blue and yellow pansies and fragrant pink and red nicotiana bring life to a patio.*

RIGHT: *These three oversized antique urns filled with pansies match the period mood of their eighteenth-century house. Lilac wisteria climbs over the back wall.*

BELOW: *Pink petunias and red begonias in weathered local stone planters act as visual punctuation to emphasize a stone gateway in England.*

ABOVE: *Alpine phlox, gentians, and potentilla are displayed to their best in miniature rock gardens created in a pair of raised stone troughs. Mustard-yellow sedum (*Sedum acre*) creeps across the gravel path beneath.*

LEFT: *Containers can be moved around the garden to add color or interest to different areas. At the entrance to a Long Island garden, landscape gardener Lisa Stamm used a pair of standard marguerites to add drama and emphasis to a bluestone path. The two Italian terracotta tubs spill over with ivy geraniums and nierembergia.*

ABOVE: *Cream-yellow 'Leverkusen,' here trained against a brick archway, is a vigorous, mildly fragrant climber.*

As far back as Greek and Roman times, roses have held a special place as a symbol of romance. The spectacular range of rose varieties, offering scents and colors in profusion, makes them a vital part of any garden plan. Many would argue that the intoxicating scent that fills the air around them from June on is reason enough to have roses in any garden.

Climbing roses, trained over trellises, pergolas or walls, will also bring height to the garden. Such a use of roses softens structural lines, raising the visual interest above the level of the borders and beds. In France a separate garden is normally devoted to roses, such are their importance, elsewhere roses are more generally combined with other plants to achieve a romantic effect. The gardener can then use underplantings to disguise bushes that are not in bloom. Even for rose fanatics, there can be few less appealing sights than the thorny bones of a rose garden in winter. Low-

growing gray-leaved plants, such as lamb's ears (*Stachys lanata*), or artemisia, are often planted to make the most of the rose colors. But it is probably more popular today to mix roses with other flowers, such as campanula, phlox, lavender, baby's breath or delphiniums, that will not crowd their June period of peak bloom, and when combined with bulbs, will lengthen the show of color.

For purer garden romance, newer hybrid roses should generally be avoided in favor of "old-fashioned" varieties. Although the hybrids are longer blooming and appear in ever more dazzling colors, they are less hardy, need more care and spraying, have a shorter life, and, most importantly, do not have the glorious perfumes of old-fashioned roses. Older varieties in nearly every case will bloom only in June (rarely, though, some will offer repeat blooms later in the year) but the bush itself will live for years and years. In a romantic garden these exquisite roses introduce a wonderful

ABOVE: *The snow-white seedling 'Lime Kiln' plays against the crimson nineteenth-century hybrid perpetual 'Jules Margottin.'*

palette: every conceivable shade of white, the palest blush pinks, delicate yellows, through to crimsons and deepest reds. Their perfumes can be heavy or delicate and range from sweetly fruit-like to spicy aromas.

Besides the color and scent they bring, older roses have pedigrees that are romantic in themselves. Many were brought to the West by trade ships in the eighteenth and nineteenth centuries from China and the Far East. Napoleon's wife, the Empress Josephine, was a passionate collector of roses. For centuries they have been valued for their colors and scents, for the medicinal qualities of their fruit, and for their essential oils.

BELOW: *In late September this bed at Old Westbury Gardens is a controlled riot of apricot chrysanthemums and coral and white dahlias, accented by lavender daisies and looping garlands of pink climbing roses over chains.*

ABOVE: *In a mixed border, the early-flowering candy-striped floribunda 'Matangi' blends happily with surrounding plants.*

LEFT: *These simple pale pink blooms encapsulate the charms of the rose.*

ABOVE: *Trelliswork is one of the best supports for climbers. It enables them to roam freely and receive plenty of air-circulation without restricting access for pruning or enjoyment of their flowers. At Crathes Castle, a cream climber thrives above the broad leaves of elephant's ears.*

ABOVE: *The full, almost pure-white blooms of the floribunda 'Iceberg' create a luminous accent in an English garden.*

RIGHT: *Trained as standards, these apricot roses contribute a formal note to the garden at Giverny.*

LEFT: *Beneath a grape arbor, lady's mantle and yellow St. John's Wort flourish next to a small pond.*

ABOVE: *Pink cosmos and masses of white daisies spill over the borders of a garden pond, blending its edges with the rest of the garden.*

Water adds new dimensions to a garden that are inherently romantic. Its sound, its reflections, the endless play of light and wind on its surface changes its mood constantly so that a pool or river brings year-round interest to the garden. A natural pond or stream, or just a plain rectangular pool, adds depth to an area and reflects light upwards into the garden. A pond of some kind is especially useful in a small garden, as it effectively doubles the space through its reflections and has the added virtue of focusing the viewer's eye downwards, away from the limited horizons and confines of the property.

In a romantic design, water is usually treated informally, introducing a sense of untamed nature. Border edgings to a pond should be in rough natural stones, and marsh-loving plants should be planted in thick clusters at its edges, blurring evidence of the division between land and water.

ABOVE: *Mixing the textures of Japanese maple, cotoneaster, weeping cherry, juniper, and mugo pines, Randolph Marshall created a naturalistic border that softens the outlines of a swimming pool and jacuzzi.*

Water-gardens introduce a new range of plants for the romantic gardener. For their exotic colors, large blossoms, and delicious fragrance, water lilies and lotus are almost irresistible. The more delicate lotus is confined to temperate regions where it receives plenty of sunlight. Water lilies can be surprisingly undemanding to grow, however they should be bought and planted in consultation with a specialist supplier. Water violets (*Hottonia distachyus*), water poppies (*Hydrocleys nymphoides*), and yellow snowflake (*Nymphoides cristatum*) also bring color to the water garden. Bog plants, which enjoy having their roots in wet soil or shallow water, are even more numerous, including Japanese iris, astilbe, hosta, bamboo, loosestrife, and some varieties of lobelia and primula.

The garden pool need not be deep. A reflecting pool can well be

only a few inches deep, providing it has a black or gray bottom to magnify the impression of depth and reflect its surroundings. Designed to capture the moods of the sky, for maximum effect a reflecting pool should be positioned so that it is naturally looked down upon. Positioning tall or colorful plants, statues, or architecture at its edges will clearly capitalize on its reflective qualities.

Fountains and waterfalls add a further architectural dimension and their own magical sounds to a garden, and are not the exclusive preserve of formal gardens. The soothing, hypnotic sound of water was well-known to gardeners in ancient times and still casts its spell today. Moving water is endlessly fascinating to look at and its sound, as any city fountain demonstrates, is an effective means of masking out the street noise for a contemporary suburban garden.

ABOVE: *Water's strong architectural potential is exploited to the fullest in a small garden in Miami, Florida, designed by landscape architects Larry Henderson and William Cummings. Using two cascading water walls and several fountains, they drowned the traffic noise from a busy highway and kept the focus of the garden within its limited confines. At night, underwater lights bring the pool and water to life.*

LEFT: *Weeping willows, rhododendrons, irises, bamboos, and huge ferns border the pool at Giverny. Trained to form a beautiful canopy, white and lilac wisteria trails around the arched bridge.*

RIGHT: *Taller plants, trees, and garden structures will capitalize on the natural reflective qualities of water. At the wisteria walk at Old Westbury Gardens, the Chinese-style pagoda entrances are mirrored appropriately in a lily pond.*

ABOVE: *Valerian, a freely growing pink-or white-flowering perennial, will survive even the poorest soil. With no encouragement it grows in the wall of a fifteenth-century garden, bringing early summer color to a shady stream bank.*

LEFT: *In a garden pond bordered with evergreens and several varieties of hostas, deep-purple irises, white aurum lilies, water-lilies, and scented yellow primula (*Primula Florindae*) flourish.*

Color

olor is perhaps the most potent tool available to the gardener. We notice it almost before anything else in the garden, and its mood—lively or tranquil, assertive or subdued, warm or cold—sets the tone for its surroundings. Imagine the chaos of a garden in which no attempt has been make to coordinate or arrange colors: a border consisting of flame-orange lilies next to the palest-pink poppies and dark-purple lupines all planted in front of a bright-red rhododendron. The overall effect would be dazzling and exhausting, but ultimately uninteresting. Like a random series of discordant musical notes, it would quickly lose our attention. For, like a piece of music, a well-designed garden explores and plays with harmonies, creating progression and variation—occasionally even deliberately setting up disharmony or counterpoints to change the mood and tempo of the design.

Color is the heart of the romantic garden, and should be applied exuberantly, lest the pursuit of harmony creates the horticultural equivalent of bland background music. Inevitably, the colors we select in a garden will create a mood of warmth or coolness, liveliness or tranquility. Besides stimulating our interest, color can expand or contract our impressions of space by altering our perceptions of distance or shape.

Numerous books have been devoted to exploring and understanding color, but like so much of gardening, there is no real substitute for trial and error and personal observation. The hollyhocks you planted last year may not turn out, in July, to be the carmine red you expected. They may dissolve into the background and not stand out as you had hoped. But nevertheless, before planting it is generally far better to plan in terms of colors—blues, purples, pinks, reds, grays, and so on—and the effect you want to achieve with them than to plan in terms of specific plants.

Every garden is a study in color in some respect. Even that so-called neutral, white, embraces everything from the chalk white of

LEFT: *Successfully mixing colors and textures is one of the great challenges of any garden; it can revive a dull corner, give character to an everyday plant, or simply add some mood. Deep-purple heads of Hidcote lavender form a feathery contrast to the green mat and bright orange flowers of the low-growing shrub potentilla.*

an arum lily or clematis to the pale ecru of viburnum. Like any
color, a white garden has to be considered along with the leaves
that surround it. The greens of foliage can range from palest celery
to deep, almost black pine and these in turn are affected by the
play of sun and shadow through the seasons of the year.

Invariably when a discussion of color in a garden is raised, Vita
Sackville-West's white garden at Sissinghurst Castle, England is
cited. Following Gertrude Jekyll's experiments with single-color
schemes, Sackville-West's design is a masterpiece whose footpaths
must be the most heavily trod of any twentieth-century garden.
Confining oneself, like Sackville-West, to a monochromatic scheme
may seem to be a simple solution for those unconfident with color.
But a monochromatic garden brings its own difficulties. A single-
color garden can become too limited or circumscribed in its interest
and be no more than a novel exploration of the various tones of the
chosen hue. To avoid this, single-color plans must invest far greater
care and ingenuity in the play of textures and shapes of plants,
which rise to prominence within a single-color garden.

Most explanations of color refer to the color wheel, which shows
a continuous spectrum of all hues including the primaries—red,
yellow, and blue—from which every color can be made. Harmonies
are formed by combining colors that are close to each other on the
wheel—lilacs, blues, and purples, for example. Contrasts are
created by combining two colors that are exactly opposite one
another on the wheel—such as yellow and deep violet, blue and
orange, or red and green.

Of course, a color wheel cannot display anywhere near the range
of shades encountered in even the most limited garden, nor can it
anticipate the variety of effects possible when they are combined,
or the effect of size of color—the impact of a large area of yellow,
for example, contrasted against a small accent of violet. But the
wheel does serve as a kind of visual guideline, which one can use
as a starting point for experiments in the garden.

While striving for overall harmony, some contrast in a planting
scheme does much to bring a garden to life. The romantic garden
tends toward more subtle colors and color combinations; brights
are often too strident for dreamworld designs. This is not to say

ABOVE: *Tiny white daisies* (Chrysanthemum vera) *and a cloud of white achillea spill over a nineteenth-century cast-iron seashell basin.*

LEFT: *Perennial borders depend on a mix of scale as much as color: a heavily-ruffled pink peony contrasts with the more delicate violet crane's bill* (Geranium ibericum).

ABOVE: *Making the most of their limited numbers, crimson petunias above trailing deep blue lobelia seem jubilant in their tiny window garden.*

that sharp contrasts should not be attempted—not at all. A particular garden glimpsed from the road once in Vermont comes to mind, where the dark brick-red house was trimmed in blue and yellow and surrounded with drifts of scarlet poppies, midnight-blue delphiniums, and bright yellow lilies. It was a delightful sight, handled with a good bit of humor, and it proved that even primary colors can look romantic, in the right setting.

The impact of a color is obviously affected by the area it covers—the more intense a color, the smaller the amount needed to achieve an effect. As a general rule, pastels and pale colors lend themselves well to planting in larger stretches—set off, of course, by the greens of their foliage. Stronger, more intense colors like the burnt orange of daylilies, the saturated reds of camellias or tulips, and the rich blues of campanulas, are more clearly delineated from their surroundings. Their impact is such that the cautious gardener might want to restrict their association with less assertive hues to accents in borders. Or, intense colors may be subdued with gentler, related shades, or with grays or whites. In a garden, too many intense colors in equal proportion, all clamoring for our attention, will be too busy and cancel each other out.

Gertrude Jekyll's designs were supreme examples of the mastery of color in a garden. She planted drifts of one color shading into drifts of a related hue, orchestrating the greens and silver grays of foliage to harmonize colors and using the strong colors as accents or as anchors for the eye. In her long perennial borders, this approach achieves a fluid effect that enhances the sense of space in a garden and fosters visual tranquility.

In choosing a color scheme, take into account whatever colors already exist in the garden site. A yellow house, for example, would probably seem more romantic if surrounded by drifts of pastel pinks and blues rather than reds and oranges, whereas a dark stone house can sustain and may even benefit from lively combinations of more vibrant colors. A brick house lends its warm natural tones to the garden it abuts, and the color of a brick wall should be taken into consideration when selecting climbers to be planted against it: if it is a dark brick-red then lighter-toned climbers would most quickly give it life.

ABOVE: *Spring colors in the garden can be wonderfully refreshing and lively after the stark palette of winter. Scattered in the grass, lemon yellows and reds of tulips hold their own against a pastel pink house.*

LEFT: *A tiny bed inset in a patio manages to make a disproportionate effect with riotously colorful pansies.*

Since all color has its source in light, the light your garden receives is a primary consideration. Morning light tends to be cooler than that of dusk, so east-facing areas benefit from a warmer palette. At noon on a bright, clear day even the strongest hues shrink from the sun's intense light and appear washed out. At dusk, the light changes rapidly, and often most interestingly, blending and melting forms and colors, softening differences; as day's final gesture, the setting sun will cast a warming glow over the west-facing areas of the garden, in particular. As the light fades, both darker and brighter colors seem as well to fade away, leaving the pastel shades most visible. Whites are the last to dissolve into darkness. Accordingly, the areas of a garden that are seen in evenings from a window or porch should be planted in pastels or whites to lengthen the time that they can be enjoyed.

Light (and therefore color) in a garden is obviously related to season and climate. Tropical light can sustain bold colors that would seem only garish further north. Compare the brilliantly-colored bougainvillea that spills over fences and roofs in the Caribbean with the subtle shades in the banks of heather that show their best in the watery light of the Scottish Highlands. A garden in a mild, damp climate, like that of Scotland, lives in soft light year-round. What it lacks in climatic extremity it makes up for in the benefits of a light that brings out the most subtle variations in color, shape, and texture.

Additionally, a temperate garden has four distinct faces, all of which should be considered. A garden with only herbaceous borders would be a sorry sight in autumn and winter and even in spring—most herbaceous borders use bulbs and masses of annuals to fill-in around dormant or spent perennials and sustain interest as long as possible through the year. Snow can be wonderfully romantic; but, sadly, few gardens are designed to capitalize on its effects. When a garden is blanketed in snow, details are obscured and the palette is reduced to dark greens, grays, and white. Thus shape and form take precedence and a romantic winter garden is built

RIGHT: *Picking up the color of the house, these lighthearted geraniums and petunias laced with lobelia and alyssum seem to be bursting from the wall. Honeysuckle grows up a lattice to the left.*

LEFT: *Against a muted background of flowering privet, Long Island garden designer Chris Becker selected an all-white garden to create an ethereal, monochromatic garden. Taller hollyhocks, plumes of white astilbe and goat's beard (*Aruncus sylvestris*), and cleome give height to the border behind snap dragons, double shasta daisies, and baby's breath.*

ABOVE: *White emphasizes the delicacy of some flowers. These crumpled white blooms on the double hollyhock 'Powder Puff' chosen by Becker have a tissue-paper quality.*

ABOVE: *Repeat flowering, snow-white 'Iceberg' roses take on an almost luminous quality in a garden border.*

around shrubs and trees with good "bones" and a fair number of evergreens. Draped in snow, the sculptural effect of their shapes or the most rudimentary topiary is exaggerated. These, of course, add immeasuraby to the spring and summer garden as well, providing the structure around which a pleasing garden grows.

Like black in fashion, white flowers are always "correct." They complement any color scheme, and can appear either simple and unassuming, as in a country field full or white daisies or a patch of snowdrops under a tree, or very sophisticated—think of white orchids, gardenias, the restraint of an all-white garden.

White flowers are as effective as the greens and grays of foliage in marrying and blending contrasting colors in the garden. As a highlight or as the centerpiece of a garden, white is even more versatile. A small grouping of white flowers will stand out amid the rest of the garden. Creamy-white roses against an old brick wall are one of the most charming garden sights there is, whereas the elegant white calla lily is perfectly at home next to a glass-and-steel high-tech home.

Very few flowers are actually pure white, however; most have the slightest hint of pink or yellow or some other color in their petals. Many of the palest, most translucent whites give the impression that the flower is being lit from behind by afternoon sun. These fragile-seeming whites are perfect for a woodland glade, where they will stand out against the darker foliage. At dusk or on overcast days, white flowers have a luminosity that brings an almost magical quality to the corners of a garden when other colors have disappeared into the shadows.

White-flowering plants probably include more scented varieties than any other color. Lily-of-the-valley, narcissus, sweet woodruff (*Galium odoratum*), magnolia, jasmine, viburnum, and common mock orange (*Philadelphus coronarius*) are just a few of the better-known fragrant white-flowering plants. For those who want to get the most out of their gardens and enjoy them during summer's long evenings, a fragrant white night garden is irresistible. There can be few more intoxicating experiences than walking through a moonlit white garden planted with flowering tobacco (*Nicotiana alata*), sweet rocket (*Hesperis matronalis*), or japanese honeysuckle (*Lonicera japonica*), filling the night air with delicious scents.

ABOVE: *In a simple color scheme, textures come to the fore. A bank of unmown grass is enlivened by a thick scattering of ox-eye daisies.*

LEFT: *The fragrant double blooms of the vigorous-growing musk rose 'Buff Beauty' can capture hints of apricot and golden-yellow.*

108

LEFT: *Because of their intense color and strong vertical shape, red-hot pokers (*Kniphofia uvaria*) are good accents for a border, almost irresistibly attracting the eye. Yellow daylilies, cream-yellow musk rose 'Thisbe', variegated yellow-green wintercreeper (*Euonymus fortunei*) 'Emerald gold', and scented Moroccan broom (*Cytisus battandieri*) trained against the wall complete this border.*

ABOVE: *In another area of the garden, lady's mantle (*Alchemilla vulgaris*) has taken over a corner of a border with characteristic vigor. Its yellowish-green arching, fluffy flowers echo the creamy-yellows in the broad, variegated hosta leaves.*

RIGHT: *Daylilies, so popular for their adaptability, have been bred in dozens of colors ranging from cream-white to deep-purple. Most varieties are in the orange-yellow range of the spectrum. This patch of pale yellow daylilies seems like a pool of sunlight in a garden.*

RIGHT: *Yellow is one of the most powerful colors, drawing the eye immediately. In the autumn border, the burnt yellows, ochres, and orange-ambers of zinnias, chrysanthemums, sneezeweeds (*Helenium autumnale)*, and golden-yellow daisies (*Rudbeckia laciniata) *make the most of late-afternoon sunlight at Old Westbury Gardens.*

Ranging from the cooler yellow-greens of some foliage to hotter shades bordering on orange and red, yellow requires a sure hand in garden planning. The yellow family of colors is energizing and inspirational. There is something wonderfully cheerful about the first yellows of spring that appear just when color in the garden is so meager. But in midsummer, when the garden is bursting with color, including many paler shades, the strongest yellows can seem brash and overwhelming.

Yellow catches our attention better than almost any color, and accordingly, bright yellow flowers advance and appear closer than they actually are. A garden full of yellow flowers almost seems to run up and greet you, and plenty of yellow in a garden scheme will actually make the space appear smaller. Because of its power, many gardeners steer clear of the richer shades, and only the bravest ever attempt an all-yellow garden.

Yet the various tones of yellow — from burnt orange-yellows to the palest butter, and encompassing lemon-yellows, saffrons, apricots, and golden yellows — are sunny, warm, and natural, and when leavened with whites or greens, are a delight. Along the roadside, even the smallest patch of orange and yellow daylilies against a dark green background seems vibrantly alive and healthy.

We gardeners often take green for granted, knowing that even if we do nothing at all, green will predominate year-round. We tend not to notice the greens of foliage — its subtle changes in hue and its textures, the effect different leaf shape or size or glossiness has on the green fabric of the garden. But, like any other color, green covers a wide range, from the creamy green foliage of variegated hostas or ivies to the blue-greens of some pines or the black-greens of certain hollies and cotoneasters.

Because greens form a kind of living backcloth to the garden, the patterns and textures created by varying leaf sizes and densities are of primary importance; the beauty of ferns, for example, is entirely encompassed in their texture and form. Similarly, the broad, palm-like leaves of ornamental rhubarb (*Rheum palmatum*) or, in contrast, the swaying white-plumed pampas grass (*Cortaderia selloana*) bring dramatic textures and shapes to a garden and act as marvelous accents in large borders. Lotus and water lilies, of course, introduce very striking foliage that provides a wonderful

RIGHT: *Blooming behind a white lattice fence, pink, red, and burnt orange zinnias echo the autumn colors of the distant foliage.*

LEFT: *Chrysanthemums come in all colors except deep blue and those we are most familiar with lie at the warmer end of the spectrum—in the deep reds, yellows, and oranges.*

BELOW: *Peegee hydrangeas, beginning as creamy pinkish-white blooms in late summer and turning a darker brown, bring welcome color to the waning garden.*

ABOVE: *Form and texture assume greater importance as the palette is narrowed in a garden. Surrounded by a tall yew hedge, a garden of only greens and blues features shaped Portuguese laurels, holly, and cone-shaped yews around box-edged ornamental beds of cornflowers, convolvulus, echium, and other blue annuals.*

LEFT: *Green is often overlooked simply because it is so prevalent, but it is the mainstay of a garden through all four seasons. The variegated color of the broad-leaved croton provides year-round interest in this window box.*

backdrop for their luscious blooms. In fact, many waterside plants such as bamboos, ferns, cattails, and irises have very strong foliage and create interesting plays of textures and forms that can be capitalized on in a damp location.

Among trees and shrubs, rhododendrons, magnolias, and other large, glossy-leaved plants create a very different look from the small, densely-growing boxwood or darker green yew which naturally forms a compact shape and takes well to topiary.

In a garden where colors tend to be softer or shapes more delicate, background foliage is of the utmost importance, since these less imposing colors and shapes stand out more strongly against a uniform and unimposing background. Privet, boxwood, and yew, with their even, dense growth, provide a good foil that strengthens a display of flowers.

ABOVE: *Color and texture are enhanced in this pairing of the circular leaves of golden yellow nasturtiums and the yellow coralline fronds of false cypress.*

LEFT: *Herb gardens are especially rich with varied leaf textures.*

RIGHT: *Compensating for its slow growth with exceptional longevity, yew is ideally suited for topiary because its compact dense growth takes so well to shaping. A garden of topiary yews can have magnificent grandeur and stateliness, such as this early eighteenth-century walk at Crathes Castle.*

ABOVE: *Startlingly blue, the papery, fragile blooms of the Himalayan poppy (*Meconopsis betonicifolia*), a perennial that thrives in damp, rich soil, have a supremely delicate quality.*

Green is the most calming color, and patches of green — in tall grasses or an evergreen — in a multicolored border will blend and harmonize contrasting colors. But green stands well on its own as well. In topiary, and frequently in shade and herb gardens, green is the predominant color. Here, the gardener is working with texture and shape, using the play of light on the leaves and shapes to create interest.

Blue is full of paradox. There's the happy blue of sky and sea, and the blue moods of one's lowest days. Blue is one of the most popular colors among gardeners, though it rarely appears in its pure form in nonhybridized plants and never in edible foods. Lavenders and purples are much more common in the garden. Historically, these colors have carried religious and royal significance dating back to the ancient Greeks, and these associations compound our sense of the nobility and stature of blue-toned flowers. Perhaps blue is so popular because it brings a bit of heaven down to earth and unites us with the placid landscapes of the celestial dome.

On its own or paled by mauve or white, blue is a gentle color that melts together easily and quickly blends into shadows (which are bluish themselves). This characteristic extends the sense of space in a garden, for a patch of blue flowers dissolves rather than defines boundaries.

Of all the colors, blue can sometimes seem to have the widest range of moods, perhaps justifying its spiritual associations. When paired with yellow, as for instance in a bright-yellow-throated iris, blue is eye-catching and intense. In contrast, a pergola or lattice draped with pale lavender wisteria is dreamily romantic and old-fashioned, and is one of the staples of a romantic garden. The same pergola covered with the lavish, deep blue flowers of a clematis would seem vivacious and almost brash by comparison.

At one end of its spectrum, blue melts into purples and mauves, creating some of the more restful colors that lie between the demands of pure red or blue — colors that are often described as romantic. At the other, it neighbors green, and this is especially visible in the cooler shades of the foliage of spruce and eucalyptus, or fescue and many other grasses.

ABOVE: *Unless forced into spring flowering, common bigleaf hydrangeas (*Hydrangea macrophylla*) bloom in late summer. In alkaline soil its large blowsy flowers are pink; acidic soil produces blues of all shades.*

LEFT: *Lobelia is one of the most popular plants for window boxes and small containers. At Spring Street Gardens, New York, its exuberant form seems to belie its confined conditions.*

ABOVE: *Its long pendulous racemes and delicate coloring makes wisteria one of the most romantic plants. Extremely vigorous growing, trained as a standard, or against a wall or pergola, it seems to epitomize the spirit of the romantic garden.*

LEFT: *Lamb's Ears (*Stachys byzantina*), a plant usually valued for its furry, broad gray foliage in garden borders, produces small blue and purple flowers.*

RIGHT: *At one end of its spectrum blue moves towards purple and then to red. Deep-purple columbines mix well with pink chives and columbines and reddish-pink foxgloves.*

LEFT: *The large purplish-blue flowers of clematis 'Perle d'Azure' smother the walls of an English house from June through to August.*

RIGHT: *Violas always seem to marry the most intense hues in the spectrum with no effort and charming results. Purples, violets, and pinks mix freely in an attractive arrangement.*

BELOW: *Drifts of daisies mixed with foxgloves and stocks form a pink carpet over the floor of a wooded area in a California garden.*

ABOVE: *Night-scented crimson nicotiana (*Nicotiana alata*) forms a vivid accent before a pot of pink geraniums.*

Daring, sexy, and exciting, red attracts the most flamboyant and self-confident gardeners. A bright-red flower will never be overlooked, and like bright yellow, brings the garden ever nearer to its admirer. City cousins to the county pink, bold reds have to be handled with care when included with other flowers because of their assertiveness, and so often find the calming influence of misty gray foliage or a contrasting dark green hedge beneficial.

But while a garden of vivid reds and oranges is vibrant and thrilling, it will not be very restful or relaxing. A deeper, more reflective palette using maroon, burgundy, or bronze-red makes for effects that are less exhausting and ones that marry more easily with other colors in the spectrum. Dark-purple buddleia, deep-red magnolia, or copper-colored maple and beech trees form effective dark vertical accents in a blue-gray color scheme. Similarly, the deep red of dahlias or the purples of some fuchsias and pansies are much less imposing than the fiery reds and oranges of many oriental poppies, azaleas, and the aptly-named red-hot poker, or some of the more saturated red peonies and tulips. These brilliant colors must be used with caution and in moderation, belonging in the romantic garden more as accents.

In contrast to the "hotter" reds, pretty, feminine, delicate pink appears the quintessential flower color. Where would we be without pink roses, camellias, peonies, carnations, and geraniums? A happy color that is pleasing to most, pink rarely has dark undertones or dour connotations.

Pink lightens a garden and adds color, lifting spirits and broadening vistas, and all hues and intensities of pink contrast marvelously with green. Coral, rose, blush, shocking, and fuchsia — for such a demure color, pink offers an exciting range of tones. Pink can stand shoulder to shoulder with almost any color, including as it does strains of both blue and red, and is the easiest of all flower colors to introduce into a scheme.

In the full sun of midday, pink is bright and cheerful, but as the sun wanes it takes on a bluer hue, fading almost into mauve as evening comes on. A very pale pink is most colorful though, in the early morning or at dusk, when the paler sunlight brings it to life and other, deeper hues melt into the shadows. Youthful, gay, romantic pink hardly needs a champion to declare her cause.

ABOVE: *Plenty of strong color can disguise limitations of space. A tiny garden places pink and scarlet hollyhocks, geraniums, and roses against the white walls of the house for great effect.*

RIGHT: *The rich, even textures and coloring of many darker evergreens are good backgrounds to show off brighter colors. The intense scarlet flowers of the Chilean flame creeper (*Tropaeolum speciosum*) appear more vivid against a yew hedge.*

ABOVE: *Pink geraniums add a bright note to this window box; in front wisteria twines around the railings.*

LEFT: *Pale pink roses droop luxuriantly over the bridge at Giverny.*

ABOVE: *Phlox is a garden staple, flowering vigorously for most of the summer months and providing massed color where needed.*

ABOVE: *Blowsy white floribunda 'Iceberg' are contrasted by tall spires of deep pink foxglove.*

LEFT: *Pink is one of the restful colors in the garden palette. A bank of hydrangeas, azaleas, and rhododendrons, all in the owner's favorite shade of pink, surrounds a secluded mossy corner in a California garden.*

LEFT: *Monet's borders were masterful exercises in color. Drifts of pale lavender irises form a pastel background in a border punctuated with intense color accents of deep purple irises, pink standard roses, and dark red peonies.*

BELOW: *In another part of the garden, saturated yellows and purple-blues are blended to create a vivid contrast.*

ABOVE: *Sprays of daisies and Oriental poppies spill out over the paths around the house.*

Romantic
Elements

Whether it is a wall to mark boundaries or a reflecting pond purely for pleasure, the architecture forms much of the skeleton around which the garden grows. This can be true quite literally, as in the case of pergolas and arbors that support vines or climbers, or more figuratively, as with a piece of sculpture or a serpentine walkway. More clearly than almost anything, these architectural elements bear the stamp of man upon the garden.

Some garden lovers complain that gardens are taken far too seriously nowadays. Perhaps overwhelmed by rigid notions of landscaping design or by bushels of horticultural advice, we have lost some of the sheer amusement and pleasure evident in gardens past. This loss of fun is visible partly in the dearth of garden architecture in the contemporary garden: where are the follies, the treehouses, the allées, the surprise gardens?

During the eighteenth century, gardening was viewed as a kind of drama, and garden architecture of all kinds flourished. Classical scenery cropped up everywhere in the form of temples, obelisks, mythological statuary, picturesque ruins (occasionally brought to life by the addition of a resident hermit), grottoes, and so on. Hermits aside, this is all too remote from the interests of today's gardener. But we might borrow some of the inspiration of this period to add an element of idealism or fantasy to our modern gardens.

Gardeners at the turn of the century commonly included a wide variety of buildings and structures that are more relevant to our taste. Often whimsical and imaginative, their treehouses, tea rooms, mazes, and belvederes were extensions of the home — outdoor rooms to be enjoyed in as many guises as possible.

An outdoor structure — whether wisteria-draped lattice, a summerhouse, or gazebo — forms a spiritual as well as physical shelter from the elements. Beyond these basics, garden architecture can exist purely for pleasure, serving as a visual punctuation to emphasize and underscore the gardener's creation. A sculpture placed

RIGHT: *Grand architectural entrances set the stage for grand gardens. Flanked by informal banks of ox-eye daisies in uncut grass, a two-storey gatehouse guards a garden of sweeping views and magnificent mature trees beyond.*

Above: *Wood gates are wonderfully versatile. They can be painted to blend with the house or left unfinished for a more rustic look; they can be ornate or simple, open or closed in design, imposing or plain.*

at the end of a long path invites the stroller deeper into the garden, encouraging involvement, observation, and contemplation. A shaded bench invites repose, as a path that disappears around a green bend compels one to explore beyond. Found objects — a piece of weathered wood or stone, for example — can also have great effect, adding an idiosyncratic twist to garden.

That a functional item can also be beautiful is at the heart of fine design, and this holds true in a garden as anywhere else. Clematis will climb a decorative wooden arch as easily as it will climb a wire support, but our pleasure is increased when the functional is given as much consideration as the purely decorative. Paths, columns, walls, and buildings become of particular importance as the seasons change, since they are so much more in evidence when the borders are empty and trees and bushes bare. During the long winter months, a romantic garden needs the interest and character of sculpture or stone work, perhaps an elegant wood archway or a meandering path.

ABOVE: *Entrances inevitably form our first impressions and so should set the mood for what is to follow. Embellishing a plain entrance with a trellis, a flowering shrub, or some colorful architectural emphasis, in the garden or at the front door, establishes an air of expectation.*

LEFT: *Within a garden, arches and gates define separate areas, giving scope to the creation of different moods. Softened by a lush vine, this wooden archway marks a transition from a paved entrance to the garden proper.*

LEFT: *Billows of the climbing rose 'Leverkusen' cover the top of this walled rose garden, hinting at the gloriously perfumed Eden beyond.*

RIGHT: *Solid doors are obviously less inviting than open gates or simple archways but often necessary to keep out animals or to establish complete privacy. Here, the white 'Lime Kiln' rose flourishes in front of a plain wood door.*

RIGHT: *Open fences like this Victorian cast-iron example mark boundaries and keep wandering animals outside without interrupting the view or imposing themselves on the surrounding garden.*

The entrance to a romantic garden needn't always offer an invitation; the cachet and charm of a garden may be enhanced by its utter privacy and unrevealing facade, which only the privileged are allowed to penetrate. Think of Alice: she had to fall all the way down a dark, dirty hole before she arrived in Wonderland, and perhaps the difficulty of her entry was in proportion to the magic she discovered within. A garden hidden by a high wall or fence, which gives away none of its secrets, can seem all the more enchanting once within and secluded from the outside world.

One's first impression of a garden is usually from its entrance or gate, though hints of the delights to come may be glimpsed through the fence or wall. A look at old illustrations will show that garden entrances were often emphasized by a trellis or an arch, draped with climbing roses, jasmine, or honeysuckle to provide a scented welcome. Such an entrance creates emphasis and expectation, inviting the visitor to come forward and explore. Since a gate is usually not made of flowers or growing things, gardeners tend to forget this aspect of a garden, even though the approach can set the whole tone for the experience beyond. A well-designed entrance seduces the visitor by promising that something of import awaits beyond. And as much as the access is either secretive or inviting, it should also be a significant transition, for in a romantic garden the outside world is being left behind.

Gates should be designed bearing in mind the fence, wall, or hedge they will punctuate. Like the rest of the garden, they should harmonize with the house. The traditional picket fence, which was built to so many varied and interesting designs, is a natural echo and companion to white New England wood architecture; an ornate Victorian iron gate would plainly not marry well with a high-tech modern home. Each entrance sends its own clear message. A ramshackle gate, half off its hinges, holds out the possibility of forgotten, informal, and natural beauty and encourages passersby to enter. A wrought iron fence, on the other hand, excludes as many as it invites, permitting a few peeks at the garden but reserving the whole experience for only those invited.

Local natural materials are often preferable. They weather well, harmonize easily with the landscape, do not impose, and, like all good design, will eventually come to seem natural to the location.

LEFT: *The muted tones of a wall or hedge are perfect foils for stronger-colored flowers. A crimson bougainvillea almost glows against a rough stone wall.*

BELOW: *Pink and red climbing roses and white 'Iceberg' roses planted with foxgloves and gray-leaved* Hieracium lanatum *bask in the warmth and shelter of a white-painted wall.*

Local bricks or stone built as far as possible in the vernacular are good choices, but take the first cue from the house itself. Remember too that the planned formal approach may not be the only way to enter the garden. An entrance from inside the house can be enhanced by framing it with a pair of containers spilling over with colorful annuals or architectural plantings of small shrubs or trees.

Having gained access, the visitor will experience a greater sense of wonder and romance if the whole garden is not visible at once. No matter how small the garden, plants or shrubs or trees should be designed to serve as screens. Thus, not all the garden will be seen at a glance; the mystery encourages exploration and, in turn, screens create various areas to enter and explore. In essence, the romantic garden should be a series of entrances and new discoveries as each vista presents itself individually to the observer.

A garden with complete privacy is indeed rare; shielded from outside eyes, one can imagine oneself in the midst of a hidden glade, worlds away from other people. In a romantic garden, walls and fences shelter the garden and its occupants, excluding the sights and sounds of the daily world. Privacy is an important element of mystery and thus romance, and the sense of privilege and secrecy it creates can enhance a garden's charm. Walls and fences are integral to privacy, defining the boundary between public and private, and the height and degree of openness of a fence or wall does much to set its tone. A low picket fence is both easy to see over and through, and conjures up images of friendly, open, village life. It suggests an unassuming informal garden where friends, animals, and children are welcome. A high wrought iron fence, however, is both beautiful and forbidding, and establishes an entirely different tone. The glimpses that are permitted through shrubs, fences, and walls arouse curiosity by alternately revealing and hiding what lies within the garden itself.

Even when made of living materials such as boxwood or juniper, a wall is the most obvious architectural element in the garden. It recreates the sense of solid rooms and spaces in nature as indoors, linking the house to the garden, and thus should be thought of in terms of both. At Hidcote and Sissinghurst the gardens were designed as a series of outdoor rooms, separated by hedges, each containing a different but related garden.

ABOVE: *Larger plants or those with strong vertical emphasis such as these blue and white delphiniums blend walls and architectural features into the garden.*

LEFT: *White picket fencing has an unassuming quality that makes it suitable for all but the most imposing properties. Here it makes way for an old tree and pink bougainvillea.*

ABOVE: *Variations on the spearhead, a symbolic protection of property, appear frequently in fence designs.*

ABOVE: *Sweetpeas and nasturtiums form a colorful carpet around the edges of this Brooklyn path.*

Natural plantings probably create the most pleasurable blend of privacy and beauty, since they are soft and add their own natural textures and forms. They also act as verdant backdrops against which flowers and plantings show to best advantage. We may long for the towering thick yew or boxwood hedges of very old gardens, but today few gardeners have the time or the patience to wait for such things to grow. Even the fastest-growing hedges will add at most about six inches per year to their height, taking many years to reach full maturity.

Very often an acceptable compromise is to use a fast-growing vine, like wisteria or ivy, to soften the lines of a wall or fence. In some gardens, this principle is taken a step further and niches or troughs are created in the wall and planted with alpine pinks, perennial candytuft, alyssum, trailing baby's breath, and other small plants.

Finally, walls and fences have benefits to offer plant life as well. They shelter the garden from wind and harsh weather and also retain the sun's warmth so that species that would normally be too delicate can sometimes flourish in the lee of a solid wall.

William Robinson, the English garden writer of the last century, complained that formal French gardens "were made for the walks and not the walks for the garden." Paths don't have to play a strictly functional role in the romantic garden, but should exploit the effect and drama of the design. Have them lead people away from the house or from an eyesore you'd prefer to overlook. If they follow a circuitous route around the property, they enlarge the sense of space and can provide the viewer first with glimpses of a focal point, exciting interest before arriving at the full view of it.

A path helps the visitor to become a part of the garden as it directs his or her passage through it, creating a pause here, changing direction, and suggesting vistas and angles from which to enjoy the garden. Like halls in a house, paths relate parts to the whole, and can also serve as common areas between the more private "rooms" that make up the garden.

Paths are the simplest and most powerful way to manipulate the visitor. From the entrance, the mood of a garden should be immediately obvious. The direction a walkway takes, and the material from which it is made, organize one's first experience of a garden.

RIGHT: *In August a wild confusion of pink coreopsis and pink rubrum lilies spills over the edges of this path, as if the garden has no boundaries.*

ABOVE: *Paths can exist without formal emphasis. Salad burnet (*Poterium sanguisorba*), yellow cat's ears (*Hypochoeris radicata*), lilies, and old-fashioned wild flowers spill naturally around rough stone steps.*

LEFT: *In a romantic garden, plants are encouraged to grow freely and are constrained as little as possible. Lamb's Ears, pink daisies, campanula, and other smaller plants are barely held in check around this gravel path.*

ABOVE: *Flagstones can accommodate plantings between their cracks, softening paths and creating homes for smaller hardy plants.*

A straight, closely mown allée lends a stately, formal feeling, and defines exactly where humans are and are not to go. A meandering mossy path or an informal gravel walk, however, indicates that one should take one's time and enjoy the sights along the way, and thus is generally a better choice for a romantic garden. A curving path also serves to obscure and then reveal scenes, inviting the stroller to find out what lies around the next bend. Plainly, a curving path to a front door is more interesting in most cases than a straight one, although if it is too curved, people will begin to take shortcuts. Don't choose contrivance at the expense of practicality.

Surfacing for paths, of course, is varied. Ideally, the romantic gardener would choose paths of a soft, fragrant groundcover like chamomile or thyme, but these are just not durable enough for most areas. Near the house or in high-traffic areas, paths do need

ABOVE: *Pink evening primroses (*Oenothera speciosa*) thrive in the sun and spread rapidly around rustic steps in a California garden, creating an informal walkway.*

to be fairly hard-wearing, although they can be planted and softened with plenty of smaller and hardier low-growing plants. With distance from the house, allow them more informality, with mown grass or perhaps irregular stone to suggest entry into a wilder area.

Brick is easy to walk on and in no way hinders one's progress around the garden. The patterns in which they can be laid are numerous—in herringbone or basketweave, for example—and any pattern can be interspersed regularly with pebbles or shells, or rock set into cement to add further decoration. Gravel of various colors can seem less formal but needs greater upkeep than stone. A different experience is created with stepping stones, which slow one's progress and create a still less formal effect.

Small, low-growing plants that would be dwarfed in a large border belong next to a path and should be encouraged to spread and seed generously. Low-growing scented varieties like violets and lavender and night-scented stock (*Matthiola longipetala*), which will sweeten evening walks, will enliven any path.

Generally, the path should blend and meld at the edges with the garden itself, dissolving the division between manmade and natural. Paths that have flowers and plants overflowing their borders and spilling out into the passageways have a sense of abundance and comfort, as if the flowers were reaching out to embrace the passerby. Sharp edges, by the same token, tend to make a garden seem smaller and more formal, as well as clearly revealing the human hand in the garden's growth.

Paths can meander and wander and lead to focal points—views, outdoor structures, special plantings—and once the visitor arrives, a seat invites him or her to linger. Whether it is positioned for a small "portrait" or for a view, having a seat partially hidden by plantings or set beneath a sweetly scented arch makes it all the more inviting. Seclusion, quiet, even secrecy add to its charms and appeal. More than paths, a chair or a bench allows the garden designer to position the viewer to reflect on a scene or reveal the garden from a new angle. More sociably, it encourages people to entertain at that spot and so some of the prettiest, most decorative flowers should grace this area.

ABOVE: *A formal stone balustrade marks the border of the upper level in a garden.*

RIGHT: *Yellow sedum (*Sedum acre*) is an invasive creeper that quickly establishes itself in crevices, softening walls and paths while producing a mass of mustard-yellow flowers.*

LEFT: *Low-growing convolvulous, daisies, crane's bill, rock roses, and other perennials spill over the stone walls and steps in an informal area of a garden.*

RIGHT: *Masses of old-fashioned flowers and herbs, sweet rocket, asparagus, columbines, thistles, and the invasive herb robert (*Geranium Robertianum*) weave a verdant tapestry around this garden path.*

FAR LEFT: *A small rustic wood seat is made to seem all the more romantic and remote by overwhelming it with masses of flowers.*

NEAR LEFT: *A small white cast-iron loveseat decorated with a grapevine motif is an inviting resting point on a brick path.*

FAR LEFT: *In a glade at the far end of a garden, this hammock provides a shady place to read a book.*

NEAR LEFT: *Hung from a porch, a rustic Adirondack two-seater is positioned to take advantage of the late-afternoon sun.*

RIGHT: *Set into a mellow-colored stone scalloped niche, a semi-circular Arts and Crafts-style seat is a decorative ending point for a stone path.*

ABOVE: *With its view across Long Island Sound, a simple white bench is a popular spot in summer for relaxing.*

There is an increasing variety of garden furniture today, reviving historical styles and designs as well as offering modern interpretations of old themes. A rustic home with a wild garden might suggest a twisted willow bench, while a more formal house and garden are apt spots for the curving classical line of a Lutyens bench. Wood is the most versatile and comfortable natural material, and weathers to a lovely patina. Iron and stone have the drawback of being extremely heavy, and thus once placed are relatively permanent, but they certainly offer solidity. Stone, in particular, approaches the sense of an actual structure within a garden rather than serving merely as furniture.

RIGHT: *A plain stone slab set into a cottage garden wall and softened with a thick carpet of flowers makes a secluded resting area.*

BELOW: *Fragrant arches of the vigorous-growing pink 'Macrantha' and red 'Chianti' roses are a colorful screen for a seating area.*

ABOVE: *Shading a circular brick path at the center of a garden, masses of the creamy-white, fragrant 'City of York' rose ramble over a wood pergola.*

Variations on the same theme, arbors and pergolas are structures for climbing plants which double more or less as outdoor enclosures. The arbor is the simplest form, essentially a large hoop over and around which climbers can grow. Arbors are often punctuations for entrances. A pergola is an extended version of an arbor, covering a section of path or walkway.

Dating back in some form or another to the Egyptians, arbors and pergolas provide shade, privacy (to a small extent), and height in a garden. Built of anything from wire mesh to painted wood or unfinished rough branches—or even from cement—they can appear quite rustic or they may be highly formal, when for example they follow a neo-classical style.

As links between garden areas, arbors and pergolas shelter walks

ABOVE: *Archways can be used to mark transitions in the garden as well as provide convenient support for climbing roses and an old lilac bush.*

RIGHT: *On a property designed by Stewart Associates, a modern concrete pergola is heavily entwined with rapidly-growing trumpet creeper to provide added screening for a pool.*

160

LEFT: *A rustic wood pergola is a transition between two areas in a New Jersey garden.*

BELOW: *Arches and pergolas, by adding height, change our perspective in a garden. Above a border of white phlox, roses, and salvia with blue delphiniums, white clematis and 'New Dawn' roses form a romantic arch.*

RIGHT: *Most fruit trees take well to training. They were commonly shaped into espaliers or tunnels in older gardens as much to make them easier to grow and pick as for decorative reasons. Here, a seventy-year-old arbor of apple trees forms an arched tunnel over a gravel path.*

dappled with an enchanting light that is especially inviting in mid-summer, when it provides a release from the heat of midday. A seat or bench shaded by a rose-covered arbor is the height of romance and sensual delight.

Open-work walls of lath or trellises are suitable as both screens, perhaps to disguise a driveway or parking area, and as supports for climbing plants. Positioned to define a patio or porch or to separate a kitchen garden from the garden proper, a trellis offers the kind of partial view that piques one's curiosity, cultivating the sense of mystery that is so much a part of romantic gardening.

NEAR RIGHT: *Like all of man's additions in the romantic garden, sculpture should not jar with the natural surroundings of trees and plants. Slowly enveloping and absorbing it into the garden, heavily-scented honeysuckle climbs upwards over this stone torso in a garden designed by Lisa Stamm.*

FAR RIGHT: *A traditional Japanese tachi-gata-style stone lantern marks the entrance to an area of Japanese trees and plants in this New Jersey garden.*

LEFT: *Almost like "found objects," fallen trees, remnants of buildings or walls, or natural elements can be employed as focal points or even as some form of sculpture in a romantic garden. Here a large boulder unearthed during excavation stands poised on the edge of a swimming pool designed by Randolph Marshall.*

NEAR RIGHT: *Traditionally a symbol of watchfulness, a stone dog here stands guard and proffers a gift to all who pass through the french windows of this Manhattan terrace.*

FAR RIGHT: *Forming the centerpiece of a flower bed, a stone cherub crouches over a bird bath.*

Sculpture is possibly the most personal element one can install in the garden; thus it is difficult to offer guidelines for its use. All kinds of stone mythological figures and creatures were once quite common in gardens, but the popularity of garden sculpture has waned and so has our familiarity with their classical references. Yet sculpture does have an important place in the romantic garden, both for its artistic qualities and its role as a focal point for a lawn, path, or flower bed.

LEFT: *Only in a garden can a sundial not seem an anachronism, for here truly is progress still dependent on the movement of the sun. In a garden designed by Chris Becker, drifts of white daisies and cleome lead towards a sundial standing in front of a misty-blue hydrangea.*

BELOW: *Deep-blue Chinese bell flowers (*Platycodon grandiflorum*) and daisies almost overtake the bronze face of a sundial.*

The natural materials of most sculpture take well to the outdoor environment, weathering and blending in with the surroundings, and it was this as well as sculpture's stateliness that made the classical and mythological figures so popular in gardens past. To stumble across the figure of Pan quite literally hidden in a glade is an amusing and delightful experience.

Modern sculpture, or simply "found objects," can be placed much like urns or raised vases, sundials, astrolabes, birdbaths, and so on to add height to a design, create an interest, or offer an element of quirky surprise. Statues placed at the meeting points of paths give a feeling of having arrived, and when placed in a hidden cranny or amidst a favorite flower bed, they suggest that this is a place to linger and enjoy.

ABOVE: *Overgrown with chives,
deep-purple columbines, and yellow
fumitory lupea, an anvil remaining from
a two-hundred-year-old blacksmith's
shop is now a sculptural reminder of a
garden's past.*

RIGHT: *Pink and red rhododendrons
form a floral niche for one of a pair of
fierce-looking half-dogs–half-lions
guarding the lawns at Old Westbury
Gardens.*

ABOVE: *Blending the building into the surrounding garden, landscape architect Randolph Marshall designed an English-style thatched pool house for a garden in Connecticut.*

Gazebos are summer rooms that can be large enough for a couple, or grand enough for ten to tea. Summerhouses and gazebos are now returning to popularity for good reason: enjoyable almost year-round, they epitomize the virtues of designing for an all-seasons garden. There can be few more evocative experiences than the smells and sounds of a spring rainstorm enjoyed from the protection of a lattice-walled summerhouse, or a leisurely meal taken outdoors in its cool shade. In general, gazebos are situated to take advantage of a view, whereas summerhouses, with their more complete walls, should be sited for seclusion and privacy, so that a book may be read in peace and an idle afternoon spent without disturbance.

LEFT: *An old wellhead became a feature of the garden after it was softened with plantings of hollyhocks and a container of geraniums.*

RIGHT: *Gazebos and summerhouses should be positioned for a view or seclusion. Using wood columns salvaged from an old porch, this gazebo has both. In autumn it is perfectly positioned for enjoying the changing foliage in the Hudson Valley.*

LEFT: *Architectural elements can impose strong shape on a garden. A tiered stone dovecote forms a towering focal point, contrasting with the solid geometry of the severely-trimmed hedges below.*

ABOVE: *Summerhouses and gazebos are places for contemplation and relaxation. This thatched summerhouse, usable year-round, is situated to take advantage of sweeping views.*

LEFT: *A shelter for tender plants, the fuchsias 'Checkerboard,' 'Lye Unique,' 'Orange Cascade,' and bi-colored pink geraniums 'Frank Headly' line the walls of a greenhouse.*

RIGHT AND BELOW: *Nature reclaims all, but in a romantic garden this process of change and decay can actually be encouraged to create an aura of nostalgia rich with romantic allusions.*

The Garden Indoors

ABOVE: *Part outdoors, part indoors, the sheltered comfort of a screened porch is a place to relax and enjoy the garden. All the scents and colors, sounds and moods of a garden can be enjoyed.*

RIGHT: *The muted colors of dried flowers have a richness and subtlety that pairs well with antiques. A bunch of long-stem roses held with a satin ribbon hangs over a Victorian mantel next to an antique hand-painted mirror.*

othing brings life and color and a wonderful sense of luxury and serenity to a room like fresh flowers. In a bedroom, or bathroom they introduce warmth and romance; in a hallway, a dried arrangement offers a permanent welcome to visitors; on a dining table, they make any meal special.

Indoors, the romantic can work with Nature in a more controlled way—changing vase color, height or shape; cutting stems; mixing different blooms; moving the arrangement about a room. The effect of flowers indoors is not dependent on scale—a single bloom in a vase can be just as striking as a full bouquet—or expense—a few wildflowers gathered in an old jar will add a charming country note.

Fresh water, a stable temperature, and light (direct or indirect, depending on the type of flower) are all that flowers need to survive indoors. To keep cut flowers rejuvenated, edit them at least once a day, removing those that are too faded, peeling away old petals to reveal fresh inner ones, rinsing stems, and adding fresh water. Some flowers fade more quickly than others and may have to be removed within a day or two; as dead flowers are eliminated and the arrangement is diminished, change to a smaller vase and re-arrange the remaining blooms.

Water is vital to maintaining and rejuvenating the life of cut flowers; do change it every day at least to keep it from becoming foul. Most flowers will survive longer in cool, stable temperatures. Some flowers may even benefit from an additional soak in cool water for a few hours, which benefits blooms and leaves as well as the stems. Rhododendrons, peonies, and some orchids respond well to this form of rejuvenation, especially when they have just been bought and may have been out of water for a few hours. For flowers with delicate blossoms that tend to wilt or those whose heads might droop—like roses, peonies, and violets—an overnight soak in a tub of cool water can restore their character and keep them looking spirited and in full color. In this case, immerse the entire flower, bloom and all.

Stems should always be cut at an angle with a sharp knife (avoid scissors which pinch the stems cutting off water intake) and then immersed in water where they may drink as though through straws for a few hours before you begin arranging. Remove damaged and excessive foliage before starting any arrangement.

ABOVE: *A summer straw hat trimmed with paper flowers forms a midsummer's still-life next to a basket of shells collected from the beach.*

RIGHT: *Bright-white paint blends a summer deck with a seashore house and in warm weather becomes a gathering point. Small containers of mixed fresh-cut flowers add bright color and hints of the garden beyond.*

Some flowers need extra care. When working with tough, fibrous, or woody stems—like sprays of leaves or spring blossoms, roses, lilac, honeysuckle, or even chrysanthemums and marguerites— mash or split the bottom two to three inches of the stems and scrape off an equal amount of bark. The stems of poinsettias, hollyhocks, euphorbias, and poppies exude a vital thick white sap when cut, so their stems should be sealed, either over a flame or by dipping them for a few seconds in boiling water.

While flowers flatter any room, incidental arrangements like the discovery of flowers in unexpected places cast powerful impressions. Flowers don't always have to be used in profusion, but several small arrangements throughout the home—by an entrance, in the kitchen, on a bedside table, next to an armchair—can be just as effective. Similarly, several bunches in unexpected places: a bunch of fresh-cut flowers on the summer porch; little bouquets in guest rooms; or simple, sweet-scented flowers in the bathroom— create a luxurious feeling. Float petals or buds that have broken off their stems in pretty bowls and leave them on a bedside table.

Flowers of the same variety are generally far more friendly to adventurous color combinations. A bunch of snapdragons of all colors of the rainbow, for example, will happily sit together; simi-

178

RIGHT: *Luxurious diaphanous drapes alongside these open terrace windows are billowy harbingers of every breeze.*

larly a posy of pansies in their deep, strongly contrasting hues makes a wonderful splash on a summer windowsill.

The romantic pursues elusive qualities in an arrangement, always trying to capture the delicate and unique beauty of the individual flowers and combine them in a beautiful result. A further dimension to any selection is added by scent. Scent is one of the most powerful charms of flowers and should play a key part wherever possible: lillies of the valley, freesia, lavender, lemon geranium, sweet peas, old-fashioned roses, and French lilac add immeasurably to their appeals with their exquisite fragrances.

Whether you make flowers and their containers focal points or let them echo and play off the fabrics and colors, they should be placed where they can best animate the room. If they are on a window ledge in direct sun, they will tend to dissolve in the bright

FAR LEFT: *Outdoors, a table covered in fresh white linen and best silver is a perfect setting for a summer lunch. Mauve roses against white delphiniums are the centerpiece for two pink arrangements using phlox, cosmos, and other fresh-picked garden flowers.*

NEAR LEFT: *A white lattice outdoor room in summer becomes a place for breakfast and afternoon teas.*

FAR LEFT: *In June, when the beds of perennials on this Manhattan terrace are at their peak, fresh flowers can be gathered to add to store-bought orchids for indoor arrangements.*

NEAR LEFT: *Generous wicker chairs covered in summery white cotton fill a long porch shaded from the midday sun.*

light. Subtle hues and shapes benefit from gentle, soft light where they can stand out. Don't hide them in a dark corner though; instead, give them soft, indirect light to play up their colors and textures, or set them in front of a lace-curtained window so they can flourish in dappled sun. Place them against simple backgrounds where they will stand out more strongly, or put them in front of a mirror—or two—they'll be more prominent and look lusher. On a glass tabletop they'll seem airier, almost floating. An antique lace dresser scarf or snowy linen tablecloth will reflect light up under the arrangement. If you can't find a pretty vase, wrap any container in lace or linen (or even cheesecloth) and tie a thin velvet ribbon or satin cord around it. Or use heavy white or foil paper tied with gold cord. Smaller flowers, such as pansies, miniature roses, or violets will come to life against a lacy paper doily.

There are no strict rules to flower arranging as it is practiced in the West. Rather, it is a skill learned as mostly by trial and observation. Romantic effects normally rely on a more informal approach, where the flowers are allowed to express their particular character, rather than being forced or manipulated to fit a prescribed design. In keeping with this informality is a free use of materials—foliage, twigs and grasses, mosses and ferns, even found objects like shells, stones, or driftwood, besides the flowers themselves.

To begin with, the flowers should be chosen with a setting or occasion in mind. Bear in mind the color scheme and furnishings of the room, as well as the color, scale, and shape of the container. For example, the lines of a tall, elegant vase are more visible and can be enhanced by filling it with taller arching flowers or sprays of blossom; the centerpiece for a formal dinner party should be more imposing than that for a picnic; or an arrangement for a sitting room larger than one for the kitchen windowsill.

As outdoors, it is the range and mix of colors that brings most excitement and interest to a selection of flowers; their shapes and textures are important but subsidiary. In the smaller scale of an arrangement, the principles of color harmony are perhaps even more significant than in the more generous spaces of the garden, where they have more room to breathe. Dividing the color wheel into warm and cool colors is a simple means of analyzing which colors will most readily marry well and which will be more inclined

to conflict. The warmer half of the spectrum includes scarlet, orange, yellow, and yellow-green (all colors that contain yellow); cool colors contain blue and include crimson, violet, indigo, and blue-green. Harmonious combinations are far easier to create using colors only from one side of the wheel; contrasts are most simply created by mixing warm and cool colors.

Begin by choosing a basic color scheme, which could be based on the container you wish to use or the colors in the room or simply the flowers that are looking best in the garden. With this as a starting point, add contrasting colors progressively to increase interest or introduce some mood. For example, a bunch of bright yellow daffodils will be enlivened by adding some deep-blue irises; that is, by adding some cool colors to a warm color scheme. Contrasts have to be handled with care, however; if too many irises are added, the blue will begin to neutralize its opposite—yellow—and the two warring colors will effectively neutralize each other. But contrasts of color or shape or texture can be the life of an arrangement. The spark created by them is often quite disproportionate—one or two contrasting colors will bring to life plain flowers.

LEFT: *A plain tiled roof against a garden wall forms a shelter for an assortment of bamboo furniture. Pink and cream-white climbing roses tumble over the roof above.*

186

Sometimes a particular room or situation demands a simple, strong color scheme. Many bathrooms, for example, are predominantly white or almost monochromatic—gray or pink—and flowers need to be bold and cheerful to soften the numerous hard surfaces and hold their own. Combining flowers of the same or closely related colors—rose-pink peonies and tulips, for example—will very simply create a bold arrangement that will make a powerful impact on a room. In such a monochromatic arrangement, shapes and textures become more prominent, and should be harmonious but still varied enough to create some interest.

Still, our inclination is to reach for the brightest, most saturated colors to create an impact. But while a bowl of bright orange zinnias or sky-blue delphiniums will draw our attention almost inevitably, mixing in other colors produces a result with more lasting interest. Whites and the grays and greens of foliage will act as foils and moderate some of the more assertive colors. Intense colors can be subdued and tamed with a background of foliage; more delicate flowers need a neutral background to highlight their miniature charms. Lily-of-the-valley, for example, gains strength and comes to life when arranged in a posy against its broad green leaves.

Choose greens as imaginatively as the flowers themselves, and experiment with alternatives to maidenhair ferns—ivy and vinca, eucalyptus, variegated hostas or hollies. For more vertical accents include grasses, bamboos, or spikey, silvery thistles; more dramatic still are rhubarb and cabbage leaves.

Besides serving as a natural background for colors, foliage adds texture. Ferns and grasses will contribute taller feathery outlines to an arrangement. In contrast, the broad glossy leaves of rhododendrons and magnolia or the mat foliage of hostas will add bulk and solidity and more naturally belong in the center of a design.

Grays have the effect of intensifying colors, just as the slivery palettes of Dusty Miller (*Senecio cineraria*) and artemesia are perfect foils for the voluptuous colors in a rose garden, so gray foliage will add an extra spark to the color in a floral array. A bunch of lavender, some sprigs of eucalyptus, or one or two broad gray mullein leaves will make colors "jump" a little more.

RIGHT: *In large rooms, smaller arrangements should be positioned where they can be enjoyed fully. Here pink orchids and ruffled godetia are placed next to a favorite chair.*

While color establishes the predominant mood of an arrangement and is usually the first thing we notice, scale and shape of the design and the individual components are essential aspects of a successful effect. Flower shapes, like their colors, can be harmonious or contrasting—compare the simple daisy forms of flowers with the trumpet shapes of lilies, foxgloves, spikes of lavender, or loosestrife. A selection of all one shape would have a harmony but not be very exciting. Mixing the scale and shapes of the flowers, like mixing colors, will set up contrasts and make for a more pleasing result. At the same time, the overall shape of the arrangement is important. In outline, it can be symmetrical or asymetrical, but it should have some kind of balance based on scale and proportion. Plainly, larger blooms, such as hydrangeas or rhododendrons, belong at the base where they provide a strong foundation. Taller, less compact elements such as branches of spring blossoms or grasses will add height to a display but should not be allowed to make it become lopsided. In large arrangements, smaller flowers should be near the front or around the rim of the container so that they can be seen clearly and are not crowded out.

Make the most of the shapes of stems—longer stems may need to be trimmed to keep the design compact and effective but in larger arrangements or taller vases it may be better to preserve the arching shapes of branches or flowers. Although it is easiest to keep an arrangement compact for a strong effect, never crowd flowers—there is a great romanticism in abundance but not if the cost is that they all seem cramped. Flowers should spill over the edges of the container, appearing as if they are unconfined. If too many are squeezed into a small space the effect is the opposite of that intended, so when in doubt, remove flowers and simplify.

By changing the height or shape of a flower with careful pruning—particularly larger flowers with multiple blooms—you can sometimes rediscover a flower and give it unexpected character. Tall flowers like delphiniums, stocks, and snapdragons can be reshaped by cutting off some of their stalks or thinning out some of the buds at the center. Equally, some of the bigger chrysanthemums may quickly dominate everything around them so that it is almost better not to introduce flowers that compete with them but use foliage or grasses as counterpoints to their strong shapes.

LEFT: *A tall arrangement of mini-gladiolus is kept simple to preserve the delicacy of the flowers and bring lightness to the room.*

ABOVE: *Placed on a window ledge, a single purple euphorbia appears precious and jewel-like against the light.*

LEFT: *A bunch of cream-white hydrangeas glows in early morning sunlight flooding through a bedroom window.*

LEFT: *Entrances and hallways are wonderful settings for memorabilia and collections of knick-knacks, picture frames, lace, and other home touches. A pitcher spilling over with delphiniums and cosmos brings the scene to life.*

ABOVE: *Though it is completely without any living element, this arrangement is sweetly evocative of summer.*

RIGHT: *In the corner of a bedroom, a pebble glass bowl brimming with miniature roses brightens a rusty-orange and brown array of dried hydrangeas and grasses.*

LEFT: *Feathery wild flowers, gathered in a glass vase, are a delicate contrast to this Victorian marble fireplace.*

RIGHT: *Ranunculus, one of the most vivid and beautiful of early summer cut flowers, can combine well in formal and informal arrangements, perhaps showing its kinship to the buttercup.*

ABOVE: *Hung in a guest room, a bouquet of dried roses in a bark wrapping is a thoughtful and decorative gesture.*

Dried flowers have a sort of brittle beauty and wonderful palette for arrangements indoors. They require little care after drying and can survive even the most drafty hallway or unfriendly treatment. Most flowers need only to be air-dried for a couple of weeks before they will be able to grace a room for an indefinite amount of time. Dried flowers are seasonless; they bring images of colorful gardens and warmth into the home even when the garden is frozen and snow-covered.

Choose flowers in full bloom for drying and discard imperfect blooms or leaves. It is best to pick your flowers when the weather is dry, so that they are free from dew or rain. Avoid placing the flowers in direct sunlight; otherwise their colors will fade.

All that is required for air-drying is a dark, dry, well-ventilated place. To hang-dry, strip the leaves from the first few inches of each stem and bunch together a few flowers with an elastic band. Do not crowd too many flowers in a bunch: the air should be able to circulate around them. Hang the flowers until they feel dry and crisp—a few days to a few weeks, depending on the type of flower.

Flowers with very delicate heads can be air-dried upright to preserve them better. Leave them standing in a container with a little water until they are crisp to the touch. For full-bloom roses, peonies, and other flowers with heavy heads, laying them flat on mesh screens or brown paper is the best method. To keep the full shape of the blooms, slip the stems through the wire mesh so the petals will not be squashed.

ABOVE: *The palest cream-whites of hydrangeas and the spiky brown heads of thistles form part of a sepia vignette on a side-table.*

Almost any mixture of fragrant herbs, spices, and flowers is suitable for making dry potpourris. For infusions of color, use roses and pansies; for fragrance, lavender, violet, and chamomile. Spices like cinnamon, ginger, cloves, and allspice are good staples as are the scented leaves of rose geranium, basil, eucalyptus, lemon balm, rosemary, tarragon, and thyme. Dried pieces of citrus peel will also add longlasting scent to a mix. To further preserve the scent of a potpourri mix, add chopped orris root and gum benzoin, available at most botanical suppliers.

There are as many kinds of potpourri as your ingenuity can devise. Some potpourri recipes even span generations, but try experimenting. Part of the pleasure of potpourri comes from the charm of the container itself. Look in the kitchen and dining room for more imaginative ideas: a soup tureen or decorative casserole—even a soufflé dish—or a copper fish poacher, virtually any silver serving piece; cache pots or primitive wooden bowls; delicate teacups and saucers, crystal water goblets, or elegant vodka glasses can be ideal.

Sachets are a romantic way to scent linens in drawers, closets, or trunks, especially when they are in decorative bags, perhaps made from lace handkerchiefs or scraps of old linens. Sachets also make wonderful gestures and greetings when tied to doorknobs or bedposts. The true romantic, of course, can't resist tussie mussies—little bouquets of floral messages that were passed between friends and lovers in the nineteenth century as tokens of affection. The secret of these arrangements was rooted in the meaning of each flower. While each flower conveyed a different sentiment, tussie mussies always contained at least one rose—love.

Pomanders are also romantic additions indoors. Any citrus fruit pressed with cloves and rolled in a mixture of allspice, cinnamon, ginger, nutmeg, and orrisroot becomes a lasting ornament that also scents closets or drawers.

ABOVE: *The rose potpourris at Spring Street Gardens are stored in simple wicker baskets that allow the full fragrance of the scented mixtures to be released.*

RIGHT: *Roses are always a good choice for drying. Once preserved, their original palette deepens, capturing much of the nostalgic beauty of dried flowers, especially when paired with an antique vase or bowl.*

LEFT: *Chintz boxes, decorative baskets, and fresh flowers mix together on a bedroom dresser.*

BELOW: *Ferns, so beloved by the Victorians, have a richness of texture and color that matches a traditional decor.*

RIGHT: *In a pink bedroom, an arrangement of fresh lilies and roses is very feminine.*

204

LEFT: *Often accused of appearing too blowsy in the garden, the fully-shaped hydrangea is more restrained when dried.*

BELOW: *Lace curtains shield a room from the worst of the day's heat, while still admitting plenty of sunlight. One or two flowers in small vases hint at the garden that awaits beyond the door.*

RIGHT: *Soft light falling through open french doors flatters a bouquet of roses and makes an armchair more inviting.*

ABOVE: *Placing single blooms where they can be caught in the light from a window gives them added emphasis.*

LEFT: *Flowers with strong lines such as these white lilies often benefit from a simple treatment that underlines their elegance. Against the light cast by a window their whites seem even more luminous.*

RIGHT: *Simple white daisies and freesias are paired effectively with small kitchen jugs and a glass carafe on this breakfast-room windowsill.*

Besides being longer lasting than cut flowers, bulbs are good choices indoors. Not only are they welcome reminders of spring during colder months, but you can also enjoy watching their progress from plucky little shoots to full bloom. Planted in the autumn in a container and positioned indoors on a sunny window ledge, any bulb will bloom in the spring, provided it does not dry out and is fertilized occasionally. Amaryllis, calla lily, anemone, ranunculus, freesia, and many other tender bulbs can be established in autumn in a cool room, such as an enclosed porch, and brought into warmer areas to bloom. The exact steps will vary according to the variety, so follow the supplier's recommendations for watering and fertilizing.

Many hardy bulbs can also be "forced" to bloom early, bringing delightful color to a room indoors even during the depths of winter. Not every variety can withstand the strain of this treatment but many narcissus, hyacinth, and early spring bulbs such as snowdrop, grape hyacinth, crocus, dwarf iris, and lily of the valley are suitable for forcing and can be brought into bloom in December or January indoors with little difficulty.

Some bulbs, such as hyacinths, can be forced on a bed of pebbles and water, but the best results come from a soil medium, especially if they will be planted outdoors after blooming. Select a container at least twice as deep as the bulbs themselves. Besides regular terracotta pots, kitchens afford a wealth of possible decorative containers, from vegetable dishes to small wood fruitboxes.

To force bulbs, winter conditions must be simulated for a period of 8 to 12 weeks or so when they must be kept in a dark, dry, cool (30-45°F) environment—a refrigerator, garage, or basement will do. (This time will vary, depending on the variety, so check with the bulb supplier.) Once roots have begun to develop they can be removed and gradually introduced to light and warmth indoors before finally being placed on a windowsill or a table in sun-

RIGHT: *Most varieties of daffodils are suitable for growing indoors and many will take well to forcing during winter. As outdoors, daffodils seem to benefit most from being grouped in clumps of half-a-dozen or more.*

LEFT: *Indoors, there are numerous effects with flowers and plants that can be adapted to the scale and mood of the room. In a large formal sitting room, a pair of topiary rosemary bushes stand as formal accents alongside a gilt mirror.*

RIGHT: *In a rustic country house, nature imitates art through this still-life of cut flowers and botanical prints.*

light, where they will be able to bloom properly. Bloom time is approximately four to six weeks after the bulbs have been brought out of cold storage.

For the indoor gardener who is tired of geraniums, flowering plants can be grown in containers outdoors and brought indoors once they are at their best. Garden flowers such as foxglove, cosmos, bleeding heart, delphinium, the colorful hibiscus, astilbe, and lupine, set in weathered or ornamental terracotta pots, make beautiful additions to any room. Even shrubs such as hydrangea, dwarf rhododendron, or a rose that has been trained as a standard can be brought to a sunny spot indoors to add color and life to a room. All the fragrant herbs—rosemary, lemon balm, lemon thyme, sage, and not least lavender—make ideal indoor plants for the kitchen, and bring garden fragrances to most rooms.

Brandy Flavored with Summer Fruit

Fresh fruit liquors bear no comparison to the fruit-flavored brandies and liqueurs available in the stores. Start with fresh fruit and a good quality brandy and it is almost impossible not to end up with something good. These keep well and continue to mature for several months, until they are strained, so do make them well in advance. Try combinations like orange-cranberry, raspberry-peach, or anise-blueberry.

MAKES ABOUT 1 QUART

---

4 cups strawberries, cranberries, or cherries

---

2 cups brandy

One Week Later:

1½ cups water

---

1 cup sugar

---

1 cup brandy

Crush the fruit in a bowl, then pour it into a jar. Add the two cups of brandy. Seal tightly and shake well to mix. Set aside the brandy in a cool, dark place for one week. After one week, complete the brandy with a sugar syrup. Heat the sugar and water and stir to dissolve the sugar. Set aside to cool. Strain the brandy two or three times through a double layer of cheesecloth, making sure to squeeze all the liquid out of the pulp. Stir the cup of brandy and the sugar syrup into the strained fruit brandy. Pour into bottles and seal tightly.

Rose Petal Jam

This sweet-scented jam has a delicate flavor that is sublime spread on morning toast or between the layers of a light cake.

MAKES 6 CUPS

20 sweet-scented roses, red and pink

6 cups sugar cubes

1 quart water

1 cup boiling water

½ teaspoon citric acid

Gather the roses when they are fully open and fresh. Heat the sugar cubes with the quart of water until they are dissolved, then boil for half an hour over medium heat. Separate the petals, remove the white base of each petal, and tear the petal in half. Place the petals in a large bowl and add 1 cup boiling water. Stir gently, making sure all the petals are thoroughly moistened, then pour the petals and the soaking water into the boiling syrup, stirring constantly. Boil for another half hour, stirring frequently with a wooden spoon, pressing the petals down into the syrup (some tend to float to the top). When the petals are tender and the syrup clear, add the citric acid and boil for ten minutes or until the mixture becomes syrupy. Pour into prepared jars and seal tightly.

Summer Melba

Fresh raspberries in January? . . . very nearly with Melba sauce prepared during the summer when the berries are at their peak. Serve it over poached peaches, baked custards, or as a bed for grapefruit sherbet.

MAKES 2 CUPS

2 pints fresh raspberries

½ cup superfine sugar

1 tablespoon lemon juice

2 tablespoons kirsch

Mash the berries in a bowl and put them through a food mill or a fine sieve to remove all the seeds. Stir in the sugar, lemon juice, and kirsch. Pour the sauce into a jar, seal tightly, and store in the refrigerator. Freeze the sauce if you wish to keep it for more than a few days.

Raspberry Vodka, Blueberry Gin

Vodka and gin flavored with sun-ripened fruit will tease and tantalize any February palate. The method is identical to that for fruited brandies, but clear vodka or gin will assume the glorious color of the fruit. Adjust the sugar for the sweetness of your berries.

MAKES ABOUT 1 QUART

---

4 cups raspberries, blackberries, black currants, or blueberries

---

2 cups vodka or gin

One Week Later:

1½ cups water

---

1 cup sugar

---

1 cup vodka or gin

Crush the fruit and pour into a jar. Add two cups of liquor and seal tightly. Shake to mix well. Set the jar aside in a cool, dark place for one week. After one week, complete the liquor with a sugar syrup. Heat the sugar and water and stir to dissolve the sugar. Set aside to cool. Strain the liquor two or three times through a double layer of cheesecloth, making sure to squeeze all the liquid out of the pulp. Stir the cup of vodka or gin and the sugar syrup into the strained fruit liquor. Pour into bottles and seal tightly.

Candied Mint Leaves

Mint is certainly one of the most prolific herbs, and April's delicate seedling inevitably becomes September's bushelful. Mint leaves are a traditional garnish, but a sugar dressing lifts them out of the ordinary. A bright, dry day is best for making these.

MAKES ABOUT 2 CUPS

---

1 cup fresh mint leaves

---

1 egg white

---

2 cups sugar

Rinse and thoroughly dry the mint leaves. In a shallow bowl, beat the egg white until it is frothy. With a narrow pastry brush, coat the leaves on both sides with egg white. Dust the wet leaves with sugar and set them out to dry on waxed paper. Allow the leaves to stand until they are completely dry, at least two hours. Store them in an airtight container.

Fresh Berry Vinegar

Raspberries, blackberries, gooseberries—even strawberries—bring irresistible flavor to vinegar. After the vinegar has steeped, strain and pour it into a decorative bottle, add a few whole, fresh berries, and label.

MAKES 5 CUPS

1 cup fresh berries

4 cups white wine vinegar

⅓ cup sugar

Put the berries in a 5-cup jar or bottle. Heat the vinegar and sugar together and stir to dissolve the sugar. Pout the warm vinegar into the jar and mash the berries to release their flavor. Seal the jar tightly and set it aside in a dark, cool place for at least two weeks. Strain before using.

Crystallized Lavender

There are those who believe there can never be enough ways to savor this exquisite herb: as an aromatic in potpourris and sachets; as an infusion in bath water; or gathered into a generous bouquet, dried, and hung, perhaps, on a bedroom mirror. This recipe brings lavender to the table, as an elegant decoration for delicate sorbets or summer fruit soups.

MAKES ABOUT 2 CUPS

1 cup lavender flowers

1 egg white

1½ cups sugar

Rinse and thoroughly dry the lavender. In a shallow bowl, beat the egg white until it is frothy. Dip the flowers into the egg white, then into the sugar. Set them out to dry on waxed paper. Allow the flowers to stand until they are completely dry, at least two hours. Store them in an airtight container.

Scented Water

In earlier times, household linens were laundered, then rinsed in water perfumed with sweet herbs from the garden. To make scented water, use herbs such as lemon balm, mint, rosemary, or sweet marjoram. Place the herb in a saucepan and add water to cover. Bring to a boil, cover the pan, and remove from the heat. Allow the herb to steep for several minutes. Allow the water to cool to lukewarm, strain it into a bottle or jar, and seal tightly. To use, pour the water directly into the washing machine during the rinse cycle. Scented water will keep for several days in a cool, dry place or refrigerated.

ACKNOWLEDGMENTS

A book such as this would not be possible without the help and support of many people. David Robertson, Alesia and Victor Kavey, Randolph Marshall, Lisa Stamm, Dan Stewart, Chris Becker, Bill Stites, Kate Zari, and Rita Bobry at Spring Street Gardens in New York City deserve special thanks, as do the National Trust for Scotland and the staff at Crathes Castle for allowing us to photograph there.